THE PRAGUE CRYSTAL

The Prague Crystal

❖

DANA KOBERNICK

This edition published in 2018 by Dana Kobernick: Montreal, Canada.
WWW.ThePragueCrystal.COM

Print ISBN 978-1-7752166-1-2
Ebook ISBN 978-1-7752166-0-5

Cover and jacket design by Josie Gold
Author photo by Pam Orzeck
Design and production of book and ebook interiors by Allen Zuk

For my family

CHAPTER I

MIA

There had been an exchange of flight information and photos. That was all. Now Mia was waiting for Jake at the arrivals gate. She examined the faces as they emerged, one-by-one, but none looked like the image she had committed to memory. A steady flow of passengers continued, some of them squinting through eye slits, their clothes wrinkled and their stride unsteady, testimony to the overnight journey. The crowd thinned and that's when Mia's brain engaged. She started to rifle through her purse fearing now that she might have missed him, or got the time wrong, or the day or – was she even at the right airport? She pulled out a crumpled piece of paper and compared her notes with the information on the screen overhead. As she did, a man wandered out, his head bent downward, his eyes locked on his phone. It was him. She tried to get a good look at his face, and wondered if he too might be anxious.

Clearly not. He was otherwise preoccupied and apparently in no hurry to meet her. She willed him to look up and when he did, finally, she watched as he scanned the area until his eyes landed on her. As he approached, Mia sized him up. His shirt was partially tucked into his jeans, his dark hair was mussed and his face unshaven. His wire-rimmed glasses sat crooked on his nose and magnified his green eyes. Mia had imagined that Jake would be taller – taller than her five feet ten inches – and she scolded herself for the upsurge of disappointment.

With two hours to kill before their connecting flight, Mia suggested that they pass the time at Starbucks, finding comfort in the familiar even though she had just left home. Sitting across from one another, her nerves, coupled with the fatigue now starting to set in, had her assailing Jake with questions about his life in New York. Her thoughts were racing as fast as the people swirling around her. Many darted in and out, getting their caffeine-fix before jetting off to their destination, while others sat alone over their beverages tapping away on their computers. Amid her attempts to curtail her own ramblings, Mia tried to tune out the loud-talkers, involved in multilingual phone conversations and oblivious to their amplified voice level.

"What do you do?" she asked. Despite her intentions, she was conscious that her questions were quickly turning their conversation into an interrogation.

"I'm in finance, just like half of Manhattan," he said, and as he did he glanced at his wrist. Mia was certain that he was already bored with her. "Oh, right. I realized when I was ten minutes away from my apartment that I had forgotten my watch. Let's go find one." Jake stood up, slung his backpack over his shoulder and headed toward the door. Midway through her Frappuccino and still trying to ease into their exchange, Mia didn't immediately move, but Jake didn't look back to see if she was following. With a shrug of her shoulders, she too stood up and, dragging her wheeled carry-on behind her, wove her way through the suitcases of other travellers that were strewn about the floor. She stumbled over a bag in her path, apologized to its owner, and then darted out the door to catch up to Jake.

As they moved together through the airport, Mia was grateful for the silence that fell between them and a sudden sense of exhaustion overwhelmed her. She could not stifle a yawn and out of the corner of her eye she saw Jake succumb as well.

Jake took his time poring over watches, trying them on, taking them off, asking Mia's opinion, trying them on again. Mia was enjoying the casual comfort that had started to develop between them. For a few moments, she let herself believe that she was part of a couple. The din around her faded and the frenetic activity of the airport slowed, as she was lulled into the daydream. She and this man beside her were on a European escapade, discovering the sights of foreign countries and discovering each other. But the fantasy was short-lived when she noticed the time on the watches that they were so carefully examining.

"Jake?"

"I think I'm ready. Look at that one," he said, distracted again. "Can I see that Swiss Army watch with the stainless steel strap?"

"Jake, our flight leaves in fifteen minutes." She struggled to maintain her exterior calm but thought she might have to bolt. As if on cue, the last boarding call for their flight was announced over the loudspeaker but Jake was unmoved. The saleswoman was in no hurry either. She sauntered to the cabinet that contained the Swiss Army watch and slid a key into the lock. She tried to turn it but it wouldn't budge. She pulled the key out and examined it, giggling at her mistake, then selected another one from the key ring and tried again. She glided the door open and pulled out a watch just to the left of where Jake was pointing.

"This one?"

"No, that one," Jake said, tapping the glass of the cabinet. She laughed again.

Jake studied it, tried it on, and extended his arm toward Mia. "I'll take it," he said, not waiting for her reaction. He scrambled to pull his credit card out of his wallet as Mia inched toward the door. As Jake completed the transaction Mia stood in the corridor, squinting her eyes to see just how far gate 73 was. He emerged with wallet in one hand, credit card in the other, and the two of them sprinted through Schiphol Airport arriving breathless at the gate. She pulled her boarding pass and passport from her purse and handed both to the agent while Jake searched his jacket pockets and his bag before finally producing his. They moved down the gangway and onto the plane, where a flight attendant showed Jake to the first class cabin while Mia was directed to her seat down the aisle.

"How about we have dinner together once we get to Budapest?" Jake asked, looking back over his shoulder, but not waiting for an answer. "Meet you at baggage claim."

Mia headed down the aisle toward her seat and stopped at 24A. She was relieved to see that the young gentleman in 24B was already engrossed in whatever it was he was watching on his iPad and barely shot her a glance as he pulled in his legs to let her by. Settled in her seat, Mia became aware of the churning in her gut. Maybe it was because Jake had intrigued her. Not that this had been a date, she reminded herself. And not that she was one to fall for men ten minutes into a first encounter. Or the second, for that matter. Or maybe it was more the prospect of what awaited that unnerved her. Tomorrow, she would be meeting the rest of the group, forty-eight other people, thrown together some four thousand miles from home because they had one thing in common. Three things, really. The first was that they all wanted to see the sights of Budapest, Vienna and Prague. The second was that they were in their thirties or forties. And the third thing was that they were all single. Mia cringed at the thought of the offending word, a label that clung to her like a second skin. Never had she thought that at the age of forty-one she would be travelling bumpy highways and trekking through foreign towns with a bunch of people whose kinship to her was based solely on their shared failure at finding love.

Mia turned her thoughts back to Jake. Not one to cling to the notion of fate, she still thought it was serendipitous that the two of them had decided to head over a day early to get settled in and, by chance, were both flying through Amsterdam. Though the trip organizer had shared this information with both her and Jake and suggested that they meet up, it had still taken an awkward minute on the phone before Jake had understood who was calling. And in that moment, while regretting making the call, Mia was sure he could hear her thumping heart through the phone. She was frustrated that her upcoming trip had filled her with dread and obscured any real feelings of excitement. Group travel was not her thing, nor was calling up men she didn't know.

And now, here she was, thousands of miles from home and her comfort zone.

◇

Had Mia arrived in Budapest on her own, the language barrier and ensuing frustrations would have rattled her. Instead, she and Jake laughed their way through the charades, sign language and occasional use of Jake's English-Hungarian dictionary that eventually got them to their hotel.

In the quiet of her room, Mia resisted dropping to the bed and busied herself instead with her usual hotel room rituals. She closed the drapes ensuring that the room would be sufficiently dark and conducive to sleep. She wiped down the television remote control and tore the bedspread off the bed, recalling a gruesome *60 Minutes* segment she had seen. Next, Mia inspected the mattress for bedbugs, wincing at the thought of what she might find. With that done, and a satisfactory examination of the bathroom, she splashed water on her face and changed her clothes before meeting Jake in the hotel lobby.

That night over dinner, Mia tried to bury her inner cynic and silence the voice warning her that these kinds of things never worked out. At least not for her. They were sitting at Gundel, one of Budapest's most luxurious restaurants. It had a kind of aristocratic majesty that Mia found stunning, with its classical musicians, antique furniture and paintings by Hungarian masters. Jake seemed unfazed by the opulence surrounding them, and was equally unmoved by the maître d's subtle suggestion that he provide Jake with a jacket to wear over his T-shirt.

"Living in New York must be so exciting," Mia said, bringing her glass of wine to her lips. "If I lived there, I'd be at the theatre every other night. I'm a bit of a Broadway fanatic. Not to mention all the amazing museums and restaurants. I'd be broke for sure. Though Montreal has some great restaurants too..." Jake pulled out his phone from his pocket and once again she was certain she'd lost him. Mia looked down at her plate and poked at her truffle ravioli. It looked and smelled delicious but she was too tired to eat. Jake seemed to be unaware that she had stopped talking, absorbed as he was by what appeared to be an exchange of text messages.

"Yes. It can be exciting," he said, turning back to her and placing the phone beside his plate. But he stopped there.

"I've also heard that it can be a lonely city," she said. Jake nodded but said nothing. "I guess I always thought that of all places, it would be easiest to meet someone in New York. You have no idea how many times I've been told that there are no single men in Montreal. That kind of sweeping statement really bugs me. I mean, it's kind of ridiculous."

Mia continued to prod. She told Jake about her job as a health journalist hoping it would incite interest. And it did, though ever so briefly. So she was surprised when Jake took her hand as they walked back to the hotel. It had rained while they were inside and the narrow roads and sidewalks reflected the glow of the street lamps. It was oddly quiet and a light fog hung in the air. The eeriness made Mia shudder and she was glad to have Jake close by, but the gesture launched the internal debate. *Why would he take my hand? Do I even like this guy?* She fought every instinct to close her mind, attributed the strained dialogue and lack of attention to his being shy, or tired, and tried to enjoy the moment. She remembered that the others would be arriving tomorrow and half wished they weren't. In her head, she drafted the hackneyed boy meets girl Hollywood script that saw her swept away in a whirlwind romance and had the requisite happy ending. And now she wondered: *could I be that girl?*

It didn't take long for the hope to dim. A forgotten watch, a sprint to the plane minutes before takeoff and a generally off-hand attitude were thinly veiled hints as to Jake's personality. During the day, when tours were organized, she and her travel mates became used to the sight of Jake tumbling out of the hotel at the last minute and scrambling onto the bus. "Another late night, Jake?" someone would invariably ask, while shooting a sly wink in Mia's direction. It had not taken long before she and Jake were labelled an item and she became increasingly self-conscious as this so-called relationship unfolded under the watchful eyes of her fellow travellers.

In the evenings, when they were left to explore on their own, Mia found that she was always either looking for or waiting for Jake. It tired her. She wasn't just tired of Jake and his absentmindedness, which made her feel neglected, she was tired of the tedious dating game that she had been playing for over two decades. She was tired of the cryptic messages that she was often left to decode. She had commiserated with some of the other women on the trip and most had acknowledged, though not fully accepted, that a lasting, healthy relationship with a man was by no means a certainty. Some of them valued their status as single women, appreciative of the freedom it afforded them. Others rejected the label as if it were a communicable disease of which they had to be cured. Mia could relate to both sentiments. But one evening, as she waited for Jake in the hotel lobby, watching the minutes tick away on the clock above the reception desk, it was her independence that she embraced. She abandoned the wait for no-show Jake, and joined some of the others for dinner.

Jake was lounging in the lobby when she returned, chatting it up with some of the hotel guests. When he saw Mia, he bounded over like a frisky puppy and, while offering up a tepid apology, told her that he had stumbled upon an outdoor classical concert and lost track of time. With rising irritation, Mia couldn't resist reminding him of the watch she had helped him pick out.

◇

It was 3 a.m. and, like every night since she had arrived in Europe, Mia couldn't sleep. She was sitting on the edge of the bed in her hotel room mentally reviewing the trip. She had visited some amazing places and connected with some wonderful people. Jake, on the other hand, had been a source of frustration. But still, they had shared some fun times. That night at Schönbrunn Palace in Vienna, sitting together, both of them rapt as dancers swept across the ballroom floor, had been lifted right out of a storybook. And the day they spent together at the thermal baths in Budapest had allowed Mia, finally, to relax.

They were now in Prague and had spent three days exploring the castle, the magic of Old Town and the Jewish quarter. Mia was most moved by that visit. She wasn't an observant Jew but had a strong Jewish identity and felt a deep connection to her roots. She was both fascinated and horrified by what she saw and learned. Unlike many of the other European cities that she visited, most historical buildings in Prague had been saved from destruction. Within the small area that made up the district, six synagogues were still standing and some housed thousands of artefacts that had, ironically, been salvaged from other countries by the Germans. The intention had been to build a museum of an extinct race.

Mia listened to the sobering words of the tour guide and felt her chest constrict. As her group lumbered through the narrow streets it started to drizzle. She raised the collar of her jacket and shoved her hands in her pockets but when they stopped in front of the Jewish Cemetery and she absorbed what she was seeing, she could not stop shivering. Twelve thousand crumbling headstones wedged into a graveyard the size of a city block were sitting atop tens of thousands of graves, stacked in a dozen layers.

As she thought about that day, she felt a chill run up her spine. Her plan to set out the next morning to shop and discover why the Czech Republic was known for its Bohemian crystal seemed frivolous now. But she was looking forward to it. She hoped that Jake would join her on this shopping excursion, on their last day, though he had been non-committal when she asked.

Mia glanced over at her sleeping roommate, Beth, watching the rise and fall of the mound of blankets on her bed and listening to the rhythmic rumblings, snorts and wheezes that had been the nightly soundtrack since she arrived. "Beth!" she hissed. The persistent feeling of exhaustion was now morphing into waves of nausea. She walked over to Beth's bed and gave the mattress a swift kick before collapsing back into her own bed. Beth grunted, turned over and was quiet. Mia shut her eyes and willed herself to sleep.

What seemed to be moments later, a loud clattering sound awoke her. Mia had been dreaming that she was lost in the maze of streets in some unnamed city and had no idea where she was when she opened her eyes. Then Beth emerged from the bathroom.

"You're up," she chirped, oblivious to the fact that Mia had awoken only because of the ruckus that she was making. Mia ignored her and squinted at the clock. It was just past eight. She turned over and shut her eyes, drawing the covers up and over her head. "I'm going down for breakfast," Beth said. "Want me to wait for you?"

Get out, get out, get out! "No thanks," Mia said.

"You're sure?" Beth insisted.

"Yes!" she shot back, a little more forcefully than she had intended. "I'll be down soon." Mia heard the click of the door and luxuriated in the silence. She imagined having a permanent roommate and wondered if a man would be equally annoying and intrusive. She had been single for so long that she sometimes feared the prospect. But then, the solitude she sometimes enjoyed would turn into a palpable sense of loneliness and she would dismiss the thought.

Mia trudged to the bathroom feeling as if she had spent a night of drunken revelry though she had barely finished her one drink. She looked in the mirror at the dark circles under her squinting eyes and the network of veins snaking out from them. I should go back to bed, she thought, but it was the last day before the flight home and she didn't want to waste it.

Downstairs in the hotel restaurant, Mia served herself some scrambled eggs, potatoes and toast from the breakfast buffet. She sought out familiar faces and wordlessly plopped down in an empty chair at a table where three of her friends were eating. As she did, the three of them rose.

"Sorry to run off," Mark said. "We're heading back to the palace. Want to join us?"

"No thanks," Mia said, spearing a potato and popping it into her mouth. Her eyes followed them out and then she scanned the room for signs of Jake. She thought about calling up to his room, but couldn't summon the effort. As she ate the last few bites of her breakfast, Mia pulled out the guidebook from her backpack and flipped to the section on shopping. There were tons of crystal shops scattered throughout the city, but Mia wanted to go back to Old Town.

When the group had first arrived in Prague, all fifty of them had wandered together through the labyrinth of narrow, cobblestone streets in Old Town, where enthusiastic musicians stuffed flyers into their hands inviting them to a free concert. Mia and Jake, wanting to split off from the herd, had entered St. Martin's Church in the Wall, known to them thereafter as the Hole in the Wall, a moniker coined by Jake. The church was tiny, the setting modest, but the music of

Mozart, Bach and Vivaldi, was magnificent.

After the concert, they'd followed the crowds into the Old Town Square. "It's like a fairy tale," Mia had said to no one in particular. The facades of the colourful buildings that lined the perimeter of the square were immaculate though they were hundreds of years old. A Gothic church, the Church of Our Lady before Tyn, dominated one side of the square and was bathed in light against the dark night sky. The Baroque St. Nicholas Church gleamed, illuminated also with brilliant white lights. A short distance away, a large group of people had congregated below a clock tower.

"What are they waiting for?" Mia asked.

"It's the Astronomical Clock," Jake answered. "Built in medieval times. Every hour, statues of the twelve Apostles emerge from either side and tell some kind of story. Come on, let's get closer."

They elbowed their way in through the crowd. Mia had to look at the time on her watch because the filigreed dials on the clock that towered above her, ironically made deciphering the time next to impossible. She looked at the mass of people with their cameras and video recorders at the ready and the buzz began to subside as the clanging of the church bells signified the top of the hour. At that moment, two small doors above the dials opened and Mia strained to see a procession of figures parade past the windows. It was over in thirty seconds and everyone burst into applause. Mia didn't quite understand the story, but caught in the excitement she found herself cheering along with the throngs of people around her.

As Mia was enjoying the memory, Jake slipped into the chair opposite her. "How's it going?" he said, lifting a forkful of French toast to his mouth.

"Fine. Just looking up where to shop in Old Town. I'd like to buy some crystal."

"I guess that's what you're supposed to buy here. Like crystal glasses or something? I have no idea what I'd do with crystal anything. What's a single guy supposed to do with crystal?"

"Well, you know, even single guys might, on occasion, have a glass of water or something."

Jake grinned. "Just the same, I think I'll hang out here at the pool today."

"You're in Prague and you're going to stay at the hotel on your last day?" Mia couldn't contain her frustration. A few days ago, under the pretense of rescuing her from the snoring roommate, he had suggested that she spend the night in his hotel room. It was an invitation she ignored since she could barely get him to commit to one day together.

Jake shrugged. Mia pushed her plate away and stuffed her guidebook back into her backpack. "Have a nice day at the pool. Don't forget to slather on that sunscreen."

As she walked through the modern lobby and out into the streets of Prague she chided herself for letting Jake get to her. It's not as if she had deluded herself into thinking that there was any-thing real between them. It's not as if she had developed any true feelings. As she wiped away a tear that had begun to trail down her face a familiar feeling took root. It was a feeling that had nothing to do with Jake. False starts and glimmers of hope that were quickly extinguished seemed to characterize Mia's experiences with men. None had shown her what it was that people spoke about when they claimed to be in love. Invariably, her relationships were short-lived, their endings explained away and justified: he was too old, or too young, or simply, he's just not the one for me. For Mia, romantic love was elusive. Not one of the other twenty men on the trip had attracted her even remotely, not that she could say why. The real, haunting fear for Mia was this: what if choosing the right man was beyond her?

Mia shook off her sadness and crossed the street heading in the direction of Old Town. She was alone, but she was in Prague, and she would not squander the privilege. As she entered the gates, she was instantly transported. So vivid were her imaginings that tourists in shorts and T-shirts with cameras draped around their necks transformed before her into figures in eighteenth century garb with powdered wigs, breeches and waistcoats. She could have been on the set of Amadeus, but the rumble of the stagecoach, drawn by four horses, was really just a rowdy group of teens brushing past her.

Mia entered the first crystal shop that she saw. Vases, wine glasses, decanters and candy dishes covered every surface in the tiny store. "Dobrý den," the storekeeper said.

"Hello. Dobrý den," she corrected herself. Mia inched slowly through the store looking at the glimmering pieces. She was drawn to a display of jewellery locked in a glass showcase and gazed at the drop earrings, bracelets and pendants. "These are beautiful," she whispered. The storekeeper opened the cabinet and waited for Mia to make her selection. "May I see that one please?" She took the sterling silver chain from the storekeeper's hands allowing the faceted oval crystal to fall into the palm of her hand. She ran her index finger over the smooth surfaces and then lifted the chain. Rays of sunlight streaming through the window of the front door passed through the crystal creating a shifting kaleidoscope of yellow, pink and turquoise. She clasped the chain tightly knowing that if it slipped from her hands, the rock would shatter as it hit the floor. And yet, under her touch it felt solid and strong despite its obvious fragility. She gestured to the storekeeper to help her try on the necklace and admired it in the small mirror set on the display cabinet. The crystal now took on a deep blue hue, much like her eyes, which were now looking much happier. She ran her fingers over it again where it rested just below her clavicle.

Mia surprised even herself as she reached for her wallet in her backpack, eyes still fixed on her image in the mirror. Buying the very first item that she saw was impulsive, spontaneous and out of character. But this pendant was hers, that much she knew. She handed ten thousand Czech korunas to the woman behind the counter, roughly calculating that she was dropping over five hundred Canadian dollars on a whim. As she walked back out onto the street, her fingers were still clasping the oval crystal hanging from her neck.

CHAPTER 2
SARAH

Sarah curled up in the club chair next to the fireplace and covered herself with the chenille throw that was slung over the arm. She plucked a tissue from the box she had brought with her and waited. The tears came slowly at first and then poured down until she was heaving and gasping for breath. Sarah's dog was sitting on her haunches at the entrance to the room. Lucy rose and with hanging head, ambled over to Sarah and nudged Sarah's hand with her cool, wet nose. Sarah leaned forward and ran her hand over Lucy's smooth, chocolate coloured coat, then taking the dog's head in her hands looked deeply into brown eyes that seemed to mirror back her sadness. Lucy did not budge, allowing Sarah to stroke her silky ears and bury her wet face in the dog's fur. One last muffled sob escaped. Lucy whimpered in response.

As Sarah got up from the chair, the Labrador stood as well with a restrained wag of her tail, trying to assess whether it was time for play. "You're such a good girl, Lucy," Sarah said bending again toward the dog to give her another pat on the head. And with that, the tail thrashed and thumped against the couch.

Initially, Sarah had felt foolish sitting down for a scheduled session of raw grief. Soon, however, she gave in, relishing those few minutes of complete release. Though she always felt sad outside of these times, she was more in control and she no longer had to subject Matthew to her anguish. It was a struggle. Every waking second, Sarah had to use every ounce of energy to rein in what felt like crazed desperation. If she were to loosen her grip on that restraint, even for a brief moment, she feared she would dissolve.

They had lost Ben four weeks ago. She and Matthew spoke of their son as a living being though he hadn't spent as much as one minute on this planet.

◇

On the day after they had found out that they would be having a boy, Matthew purchased two cans of light blue paint and began to prepare for his son's arrival. Sarah leaned against the doorframe and watched him as he spread drop cloths on the wood floor, poured paint into the pan, submerged the roller and began applying the creamy blue colour to the walls. She had not reacted well. "Maybe we should wait a bit," she said.

"Wait for what?" he said, his eyes on the roller as he dipped it for more paint.

"Matthew." There was exasperation in her voice. "What do you mean *for what?*" Matthew stopped painting and looked at her.

"Sarah, it's going to be different this time. I promise you. Think positive!" he said, turning back to his paint job.

"Are you saying that it took so long because I wasn't thinking positively? Thinking positively doesn't make babies. Any other clichés in your arsenal?"

"Okay, I'm sorry," he said. Sarah could hear the tightness in his tone. "It's just that I'm happy. I want to live in the moment, right here, right now. It's a great moment."

Sarah didn't understand how he could feel such unbridled joy after all that had happened and sometimes she hated him for it.

And sometimes she hated herself, wondering if the deadness she felt was killing whatever life was trying to grow inside of her. And so, she turned away from him, went into her bedroom and shut the door.

◇

That day seemed like a lifetime ago. She was curled up on the sofa with Lucy, rubbing her ears and listening to her groan with pleasure. "Matthew wouldn't be happy if he saw this, Lucy. You know you're not allowed on the furniture." Lucy cocked her head. "Don't worry, baby. It will be our secret." It wasn't a secret, of course. Matthew often reached the house before Sarah got home and caught Lucy slinking off the sofa, stretching her front legs with her hind legs still planted deeply in the cushions behind her. She would look at him sheepishly and Matthew would just shake his head and grumble.

The phone rang. Sarah gently freed herself from under the dog and walked into the kitchen. "Hello?"

"Hi, honey. How are you?" The lilt in her mother's voice grated.

"I'm fine, Mom."

"Really?"

"Yes, really." If her mother knew that she spent at least ten minutes every day crying, that she could not go for more than five minutes at a time without feeling an irrepressible urge to retreat to her bedroom, she would hover over Sarah and suffocate her.

"I'm going to do some grocery shopping. Can I get you any-thing?"

"I've got everything I need. Thanks."

"It's really no trouble. I can save you a trip."

"Mom, I'm not housebound."

"Have you changed your mind? About going today?" Sarah walked over to the fridge and slid the invitation out from under the magnet. She scanned it for the millionth time, then crumpled it and tossed it on the kitchen table.

"No." Sarah braced herself, waiting for the avalanche of platitudes that were bound to pour out of her mother's mouth.

"Okay." Her mother's tone implied what she had expressed in words countless times in the past month. *Sarah, you and Matthew will be parents when it's right. It just wasn't meant to be.* When Sarah's mother spewed this kind of fatalistic tripe, Sarah recoiled, feeling the sting every time with a growing intensity. After her first miscarriage her mother launched into a ten-minute discourse on why she and Matthew were somehow better off. Sarah had lunged at her mother in fury. Matthew told her to ease up, that her mother was really only trying to be helpful, and Sarah accused him of being cavalier. But ultimately, she found herself taking Matthew's advice because the alternative exhausted her.

"I'll talk to you soon, Mom."

"Goodbye, dear."

Sarah cinched the belt of her robe tighter and pressed the start button on the coffee maker. She leaned against the kitchen counter and thrust her hands in the pockets, pulling out a handful of tissues and then shoving them back in. As the smell of the brewing coffee filled the room, she glanced out the window over the sink. The yard was empty. But Sarah still saw the vision she'd dreamed up a couple of months earlier: a little boy being pushed on a swing by his father. They were laughing at a joke that only they would share. Sarah felt chilled. She turned away from the vision, filled a mug with steaming coffee and wrapped her hands around it, feeling the warmth intensify and turn into pins and needles. She registered the pain, then pulled her hands from the mug and placed them on her cheeks.

Sarah had no idea what she would do in the many hours that lay ahead of her. It was almost noon. She could prepare some lunch, though she wasn't particularly hungry. She could get dressed today.

Matthew was always so disheartened when he came home from work to find that Sarah hadn't gotten dressed. He had stopped asking her how she spent her day. It was obvious. The past month was hazy in her mind. She woke up in the morning and went to sleep at night. On days when she was feeling brave she would take Lucy out for a quick walk, but usually she let the dog roam in the backyard. For the most part, what she did during her waking hours remained a bit of a blur.

She sat down at the kitchen table with her coffee and pressed open the crumpled up invitation. When Megan had mailed out the invitations to her baby shower she hadn't known what was to come. Neither had Sarah. And now that Sarah's world had collapsed she could not bring herself to think about her friend's joy, let alone share in it. "I can't go to Megan's party," she had announced to Matthew one morning. "I can't, I just can't," she continued desperately. Beyond being in Megan's company, due to give birth in the next two weeks, Sarah didn't want to be the guest of honour at the pity party. No one knew what to say to her anymore.

"I'm sure she'll understand," Matthew had said. "I don't know if I would be able to go if I were in your place."

Sarah rose from the table, took her coffee and grabbed an overripe banana. She winced at the smell and tossed it, along with the other four blackened bananas, into the trash. She went back into the living room and sat down on the sofa beside a sprawled-out Lucy. Lucy lifted her head, and then with a heavy sigh lay down again and shut her eyes. Sarah clicked on the television wanting to see something other than the images that played incessantly, over and over, with relentless cruelty in her head. She tuned into a daytime talk show and though she heard the voices of the two women on screen she absorbed nothing. And despite her best efforts, she felt her mind being wrenched back to that idle Tuesday afternoon, one month earlier, when she was blindsided.

CHAPTER 3
KATE

I t was a lovely view. Kate stood at the picture window, her forehead touching the cool pane, and peered out at the dense treetops,
their leaves now vibrant shades of green. St. Joseph's Oratory rose
up in the distance. And just beyond, was Mount Royal, where Kate
spent Sunday mornings strolling through the shaded paths. When she
wasn't dodging cyclists careening down the hill toward her, she loved
the tranquility of the expansive park right in the heart of Montreal.
She tried now to recapture that feeling. If she closed her eyes and con-
centrated hard enough she could smell the scents of summer and hear
the gravel crunch under her shoes. For a few moments the punishing weight, which lay so heavily on her shoulders, lifted a little. She
inhaled deeply, as deeply as she could, and then slowly exhaled until
there was no breath left. She opened her eyes, took in the landscape
one more time, and turned around.

People were moving in every direction, with a frenetic energy,
toward someone or something that seemed to need urgent attention.
Two women, walking side by side, heads down, pored over a file folder
together and looked up just in time to sidestep an empty cart parked
hazardously in their path. Above the clamour, punctuated with mea-
sured beeps and dings, the amplified voice of an unseen woman paged
someone by name, though Kate could barely make it out.

"Why don't you have a seat?" her husband asked, looking up from a magazine.

"I'll be sitting for hours," she said. "I'd just as soon stand." She crossed her arms and stepped into the hallway beyond the curtain that was pulled to offer privacy. She looked down the long corridor and thought about the people behind the curtains who, like her, were spending hours and days and weeks and months, sitting, staring, waiting and worrying in their sterile cubicles, which, after they left, would be readied for more people who would do the very same thing. The stream of people would never stop, she thought. They would just keep coming and coming and coming.

"Hi, Kate." Kate turned and looked at the nurse walking in her direction.

"Oh, hi," she said. "Where's—" she began, but the nurse cut her off.

"I'm Lily. I'll be administering your treatment today," she said, without offering any explanation as to why Kate's regular nurse was absent. Kate sat down and laid her head back on the chair. Though she had done this twice before, it was still surreal. Her eyes followed the IV tube to its end where it was inserted into the vein of someone's hand. And once again, it shocked her that the hand was hers. She closed her eyes and enjoyed what might be her last hours of feeling well. Her mind went to her stomach and she was keenly aware of its calmness, knowing that soon her gut would be in turmoil. The irony was striking, still. This healing drug was first going to make her violently ill.

"Kate?"

"Mmm?" She opened her eyes.

"You okay?" Daniel asked. It was a question prompted by real concern but it bugged her. He was staring at her with that look that he had adopted when Kate was first diagnosed. Restrained panic. He assigned himself the role of indomitable caregiver but he wore it like an ill-fitting piece of clothing.

She had been alone that day, in the doctor's office. Daniel had offered to go with her but she assured him that she'd be fine on her own, that she was sure it was nothing. He had tried, and failed, to conceal his relief. She wasn't sure at all about the diagnosis, but she was worried enough about herself without having to worry about him.

And she had been home alone when she got the call, when she heard those words, those words that, this time, were being delivered to her. As she hung up the phone, she had already forgotten what she had been told. She stared at the piece of paper where her notes indicated when and where she needed to go, but she did not remember writing them. She had just one thought. *Fuck.* When she shared the news with Daniel that evening, she barely looked up from the peppers she was chopping. "So many women go through this and they're fine. So I'll just do what I have to do and I'll be fine too." The words were spilling out of her before she was even able to think about what she was saying. Daniel placed his hands on her shoulders. She tightened under his touch.

He had been dutifully coming with Kate to her treatments. But on this day, his presence was more irritating than anything else, as he hovered over her, struggling to find what to say. "You really don't have to wait for me, Daniel. After my treatment I want to see about getting a wig here. Why don't you come back in a few hours when I'm done?" She tugged on the kerchief that she had wrapped over her bald head. It was more of a statement than it was a question and Daniel got up to leave without protest.

"I'll see you in a bit," he said, bending to plant a paternal kiss on her forehead.

The nurse glanced at him, and he acknowledged her with a smile before leaving. Then the nurse looked at Kate, who quickly closed her eyes. "How has your husband been through all of this?"

"Daniel?" Kate lifted her head and looked at Lily. "He's been all right, I guess." Kate preferred the other nurse. She hadn't expected to see a new face today and she wasn't sure she felt like delving into these issues with this person. "I was expecting—"

"She's taking time off. Personal reasons," Lily said.

"Oh." Kate was embarrassed by the obvious disappointment in her voice and rushed to preserve Lily's feelings. "I'm sure you're great. It's just that, well, I was used to her."

"We'll get you through this," she said with a light tap on Kate's arm. "How have you managed after your treatments?"

"The hair loss was more sudden than I expected. That was a shock."

"It'll grow back," Lily said. Kate wondered how many times she had repeated those same words to other patients. Kate herself was pretty sick and tired of hearing it. "Anything else?"

"The nausea was brutal for a couple of days. I guess that's to be expected."

"We administer something along with the chemo which should help with the nausea. And I'll give you a list of foods you might want to avoid and others that might be easier to stomach." Kate couldn't imagine that anything would go down easily at this point. She used to have a healthy relationship with food but in the days following her treatment she despaired of ever wanting to eat again. Even weeks later, she still approached a plate of food like a Herculean challenge.

"Anything else? Anything else bothering you?"

"No, I guess not."

"What about emotionally?" Lily was kind enough, Kate thought, but her voice had no warmth. She was detached and brusque and Kate was beginning to feel like just another cancer patient as Lily checked off the questions she was supposed to ask.

"I'm doing fine. We're fine." Even though they had not spent much time together, her other nurse would have detected the hesitation, however slight. Kate closed her eyes again, hoping that it would put an end to the barrage of questions. She thought about her nurse, wondering what personal reasons could have taken her from her work and from being here with her today. She remembered the instant chemistry and her gratitude. *She abandoned me.* Almost immediately, Kate scolded herself for being so self-centred.

With her eyes closed, Kate faced an onslaught of images. The face of her doctor, austere and matter of fact. Her husband, trying to mask his fear. Her children, outwardly sympathetic and concerned, inwardly wondering how this was going to affect their lives. Kate hated hospitals and her first visit into the underworld of the sick had been frightening. She had tried to steer her eyes away from the gurneys and the patients wandering aimlessly through the corridors in their periwinkle-blue hospital gowns, IV poles in tow. She had tried not to inhale, suffocated by a miasma of disease. And the smell: a ghastly combination of disinfectant and decay. She had felt Daniel's arm around her. He was holding her up as she leaned into him and placed her hand over her mouth, thinking she might vomit. These people were sick. And she was one of them.

The images played like a movie on the backs of her eyelids. And each time she returned to the hospital she added to the nightmarish photo album. The extent of suffering that took place within the walls of this building unnerved her. And it struck her, that at the same time as someone's life hung in the balance, someone else, perhaps just a block away, was stewing in his car, irate that the traffic was going to make him late for his tennis game. "You know, Kate," Daniel had said, "people come here to get better. Many do. And so will you."

Kate opened her eyes, bringing a welcome end to her biopic, and found that she was alone. She glanced at the table beside her chair and picked up a fashion magazine. As always, the cover bore a photo of a woman with blinding white teeth, flawless skin and the requisite cascade of hair that fell in perfect curls around her bare shoulders. Kate was usually not one to hate these women. First, she knew that much of what she was looking at was not so much an example of physical beauty, as it was the product of an airbrush and digital manipulation. Second, she was pretty secure in her looks. But that security had begun to erode.

She started to lose her hair almost immediately and made the decision to shave it all off. She couldn't stand the idea of waking day after day to a hair-covered pillow. Like everyone else around her, Daniel had said what he was supposed to, reassuring her that it would grow back. She too responded as she knew she should. "I know it'll grow back. And it's only hair. It's the least of my problems." But the ache spread within her as she stared at a woman in the mirror whom she hardly recognized. She had lost her eyebrows and eyelashes which, she thought, made her look like an alien, not to mention the loss of her body hair which made her look like a ten-year-old girl.

Kate had experimented with scarves, baseball caps, and even going au naturel. When she came downstairs one morning wrapped in only her bathrobe, her eighteen-year-old son, Seth, looked up from his cereal bowl and newspaper and gasped. "Mom!"

"What?"

"Your... Where's your...?" Seth's face became red as if he had just seen his mother stripped naked.

"Oh, right", she said brushing her hand over her scalp pretending as if she had forgotten to cover it. In fact, it had taken fifteen minutes for her to muster the courage to emerge from her bedroom. The first time she got into bed with a bald head, Daniel's words of comfort somehow didn't match the look of dismay. He would have to get used to it, but with her son, she too felt completely exposed. "You mean I can't pull off the Sinéad O'Connor look?" she asked.

But Seth's reaction was enough to send her back to her room, where she grabbed a scarf and wrapped it around her head. When she returned to the kitchen, Seth was clearing his dishes from the table. "Are you leaving already?"

"I have a ten o'clock class," he said, and watched as Kate glanced up at the clock. It was just before nine. "I have some stuff to do at the library so I thought I'd get there early."

"Of course. Go ahead," Kate said, proffering her cheek, which Seth quickly kissed. He grabbed his knapsack and shot out the door.

"You're done, Kate." It was Lily, coming back into the room.

"Great." Kate looked away as Lily removed the IV line from her arm and consulted her watch. Four hours had passed since Daniel left. "I heard you have wigs here. Can I take a look at them?"

"Come, I'll introduce you to Helen," Lily said. Kate followed her down a long corridor and made a concerted effort to look straight ahead. A slight shift of her head right and she would be faced with a long line of people who, like her, had been peacefully going about their lives when they'd been hijacked. Kate wanted to give the hijacker a face and a voice. She wanted to *see* her cancer, *touch* it. Just because her doctor uttered the words "you have cancer" did it make it so?

"How do you know?" Kate had asked without thinking.

Her doctor had been taken aback. "The biopsy shows cancer cells, Kate."

"Yes, but how do you *know* that they're cancer cells? Well, obviously you know that they're cancer cells," she said, starting to hear the irrationality of her questions. "But can I see them? I need to see them."

"Can you see them?"

"Yes, can I see them."

"Kate, I understand that you're upset. But we have every reason to be optimistic. Let's talk about next steps."

Daniel had often teased Kate about her need for empirical evidence before she would accept something as true. She jokingly argued that death was not a certainty. "The trend is pretty consistent, wouldn't you say?" he would ask. Kate usually shot Daniel a devious grin, gratified at having seduced him, yet again, into an inane conversation.

Today, she had only to look in the mirror to acknowledge her mortality and she couldn't stand the sight. As she trailed after Lily, she resigned herself to the fact that she would have to cover it up.

CHAPTER 4

SOPHIE

The only thing missing was the white picket fence. Sophie looked like one of those women who intrigued her when she was in college, with their perfectly manicured nails and coiffed hair. At the time, she couldn't figure out where her classmates found the time or the money or even the desire to invest so much effort in their appearance. But now, she wouldn't venture out of the house without a full face of makeup, a designer outfit and a second and third look in the mirror. She and Alex had two children: Jessie was thirteen and Gabe was eight. Every summer, they vacationed in Maine for the month of August, and every winter, they headed south to Barbados for two weeks. They were actively involved in several charitable organizations and were admired for their philanthropy. Alex was a much sought-after lawyer and his success meant that they could live in a large house in Town of Mount Royal, a desirable neighbourhood in Montreal. Sophie did not have to work. She assumed that she and Alex had made that decision together, though she could not quite remember when that discussion had taken place or how it had gone.

Today over lunch, Sophie was listening to her friend Leslie's marital complaints. "I just don't get how he prioritizes things. We're in debt to the hilt and he decides that he needs a new car. We just bought the house and we have a ton of expenses. And I've given up all kinds of luxuries. He doesn't need a new car, but he wants a new car. You don't know how lucky you are that money isn't an issue for you and Alex."

Sophie tried to reel in her wandering mind as her friend continued her spousal attack. Leslie's voice began to fade into background noise. She knew she ought to feel lucky. Sophie wasn't sure that her circumstances could be attributed to luck, though she recognized that most people would say so. Regardless, luck could not chase away the dread that filled most of her days. She did not quite know what it was that she feared. As Leslie pointed out, financial struggles, so central to many of her friends' relationships, were not a concern for her and Alex. He worked hard. She loved her kids. She loved her house. Her logical mind pronounced that this should make for a life that she loved.

"There are no question marks for you." Leslie was still talking. "You know that you and Alex will grow old together. You have no worries. I'm so envious of that."

Sophie didn't have the energy to challenge Leslie's sloppy equation, which allowed her to conclude that Sophie had no worries. "I suppose we are fortunate," Sophie conceded with a forced smile. She had no idea what to say to her friend. "So how does he expect to pay for a new car?"

"We'll just go deeper into debt. It doesn't bother him in the least. Instant gratification, that's what he's about."

Sophie remained quiet, exhausted by trying to feign interest in the conversation. Leslie was a demanding friend, needing lots of reassurance, and though Sophie could usually sympathize with her situation, that day, she couldn't summon the energy. She glanced at her watch.

"I'm sorry. I know I've been going on and on," Leslie said.

"No, no. I'm listening. Really," Sophie said, shifting in her chair.

"So how's life with you?" Leslie asked.

"Good. Great. Kids are great. They're heading off to camp soon so we'll have an empty house. But it will give me more time to, well, you know, it'll give me more time to get some things done." *What things?* She was missing Kate right now. Kate wouldn't let her get away with this stuff.

"I know what you mean. There's never enough time."

"You know what, Leslie? I'm not feeling that great. Do you think we could get the bill?"

"What's wrong?"

"I'm sure it's nothing," Sophie said, brushing her hand across her forehead. "Just a bit of a headache." She felt her face grow warm and an increasing urge to flee. Sophie tried to catch their waiter's eye, but he headed off in the direction of the kitchen.

"How's Kate doing?" Leslie asked.

"Okay, I guess. So she says every time we speak, but I don't really know." The waiter emerged from the kitchen and Sophie began waving at him again. This time he came over. "Could we have the bill please?"

"Sure thing. Would you like some dessert first?"

"Just the bill," Sophie said. "Please."

Leslie looked at her. "You're sure you're okay, Sophie?"

"Yes, I'm fine. I just need to go home." Tears sprang to Sophie's eyes and she turned away from her friend. The instant the waiter returned with the bill, Sophie scooped it up and handed it back with cash.

"Keep the change," she said, already on her feet and moving toward the door. As she said a hurried goodbye to Leslie in the parking lot and sprinted to her car, she wondered what she was running from. Or to. She just knew that she had to get out. Sophie headed in the direction of home, though no one would be there. No one needed to be picked up or dropped off. No one was expecting her anywhere.

Fifteen minutes later, Sophie pulled in to her driveway and turned off the car. From the driver's seat she looked at her house and admired it. The three-storey stone cottage was large without being ostentatious. It has character, she had said to Alex, when they first saw it. The bay window in the living room bulged slightly toward the front lawn. Alex was initially put off by the lack of a second bay window, but Sophie loved the asymmetrical quality. Pink and purple flowers wound their way from the left side of the house toward the right side, interrupted briefly by the walkway leading to the front door. She stared at the door knowing that if she went inside she would see her housekeeper stitching labels into her children's clothes. This was something that she had started to do, but when Alex had seen her, he told her to leave it to the help.

"Why are you doing that? We pay someone to do things like that," he had said, brushing past her to his favourite chair. Sophie actually enjoyed stitching things, but she'd put it aside.

So what would she do if she went inside? She started the car again, unsure. As she looked through her rear view mirror, she saw that a blue SUV had stopped in front of her house. She watched as the back door opened wide and her kids tumbled out, knapsacks hanging loosely off their backs. Jessie slammed the door shut and Gabe pounded on the window with his fist, mugging for his friend.

"Hi, Mom!" Jessie was at her window. "Where are you going?"

"Nowhere. Just coming home," Sophie said, pulling the key from the ignition and opening her car door. "How was the last day of school?"

"Boring. We didn't do anything. Like what's the point of even going?"

"*Like* what's the point?" said Sophie.

"Mo-om," Jessie whined, "school's over!"

"Come on, let's go inside."

"Actually, Molly asked if Gabe and me could go swimming

at her house."

"Gabe and I," Sophie corrected. She looked up to see Molly's mother, Julia, getting out of the SUV and walking toward her.

"Hi, Sophie!"

"Please Mom, can we go?" Gabe asked. Sophie didn't have any particular reason to say no, plus she could never resist the pleadings of her son. Not that it mattered anyway. Jessie and Gabe were already heading into the house, presumably to grab their bathing suits.

"Is it okay, Sophie?"

"Sure. Why not?"

"They're welcome to stay for dinner, if they'd like."

"Yes. I'm sure that they would love that. You can give me a call later on and I'll come by and get them."

"Don't worry about it. When Mike goes out to his tennis game he can drop them off."

"Bye, Mom!" Jessie flew out the front door toward the car.

"Bye, Mom!" Gabe trailed just behind his sister.

"Be careful." But they had already piled into the car.

"Take care, Sophie," Julia said, looking back over her shoulder. As Sophie opened the front door to her house she could hear the phone ringing and the distant voice of Lydia, their housekeeper, as she picked it up. "Hello?" A brief pause. "I think she just walked in. Let me get her for you." Lydia appeared at the top of the stairs and was starting to make her way down. "It's your husband, Mrs. Bauman."

Sophie dropped her purse on the table in the hallway and went into the kitchen. "Hi, Alex."

"Hi, Soph. I don't think I'll make it home for dinner tonight. I have a late meeting. You should go ahead with the kids."

"The kids are with friends. But don't worry about it. It'll be peaceful here."

"I'm really sorry, Sophie. I'll try not to be too late."

Sophie hung up the phone and sat down at the kitchen table sifting through the mail. Everything was for Alex, except one envelope, which was addressed to occupant. She tossed that one in the trash without bothering to open it. She went into the den, picked up her book from the coffee table and sank into the cushy sofa. She turned on the TV and channel-surfed through the daily soap operas before clicking it off.

"Goodbye, Mrs. Bauman. I'm leaving now," Lydia said from the doorway.

"Thank you, Lydia. See you tomorrow." Sophie heard the front door open and close and then opened her book. Years after the Eat, Pray, Love craze, Sophie had finally joined the legions of women who had lauded the memoir as inspirational, even life-changing. Though abandoning a marriage and a career to go off and find yourself seemed self-indulgent, Sophie couldn't help but revel in the author's adventures. One woman's journey from utter misery to emotional fulfillment was what was implicitly promised and Sophie was hanging on for the happy ending.

Several minutes passed before she realized that she was rereading the same line over and over. She snapped the book shut and dropped it beside her. Her thoughts turned to Kate. Sophie had called her earlier in the day but her son had told her that she was busy. She picked up the phone, dialled, and then hung up before the call connected. Sophie hated that her friend was suffering. Even when the two of them spoke, Kate would typically redirect the conversation. Sophie felt as if she was pressed up against a glass wall trying ineffectually to reach out and touch her.

"I'm so fucking sick of me," Kate would insist. "I'm such a boring topic. Tell me something new. Tell me something different. Tell me something good." But it wouldn't take long before Kate started losing steam. "I can't even have a five minute conversation with my friend," she would lament. "It just sucks. I'm sorry."

"Don't worry about it," Sophie would say. "You just take care of yourself. I'm fine." *I'm fine. We're fine. Everything is fine.* When she hung up the phone with Kate she could almost believe it.

CHAPTER 5
MIA

Mia leaned against the doorframe of Grace's office fingering the little crystal that rested with such lightness on her chest. Since buying it in Prague four months earlier, she rarely took it off. It had become a source of comfort, of security, and because she'd bought it on that trip, it had come to represent courage. Grace had praised her for having the guts to take off on her own, and the comment had given Mia a new perspective on herself and on her travels.

Venturing thousands of miles away by herself to be thrust into uncertainty was, in retrospect, courageous and Mia did feel a sense of pride in having accomplished something that, while wonderful, had also been challenging. Since returning home, she often thought about Jake and wondered what she could have done differently. Grace had listened to Mia's story of her and Jake with a kind of girlish delight, and Mia had to remind her that it had hardly been a fairy-tale dalliance. Grace, in turn, tried to convince Mia that it needn't lead to a maelstrom of analysis.

"Sorry, come on in," Grace said as she hung up the phone. "I have an interesting story for you to work on this week."

"About?" Mia asked as she plunked herself down in one of the two chairs in front of Grace's desk.

"Let's see." Grace picked up a sheet of paper from the top of a stack on her desk. "A healthy 37-year-old man donates a portion of his liver to his sick brother and then dies several days after the surgery." Grace laid the paper down on the desk and slid it over to Mia.

"Great, a light-hearted fluff piece," she said, scanning the information on the sheet.

"How was last night?" Grace asked, ignoring the sarcasm. That was Grace. From death to dirt in a nanosecond.

"So what was it exactly that made you think that this might be a good match?"

"Uh-oh. Doesn't sound good."

"The only thing that he and I have in common is that we're single. Hardly a compelling reason to bring two people together, wouldn't you say?"

"But he seemed like a nice guy when I met him at David's holiday party."

"It's not that he's not *nice*. God, I hate that word. It's so banal. We need to move beyond nice, don't you think?"

"Nice is a good place to start," Grace said. "Besides which, I don't imagine that one dinner together can be all that revealing. Do you think he saw all that you are? You've got to stop wondering whether the man sitting in front of you is the one waiting for you at the end of the aisle. You're sabotaging your own happiness."

"Don't lecture me, Grace. Please. You have no idea what it's like out there. How much dating did you do before you and David got married?" She didn't wait for an answer. "I'm exhausted. I can't go through these interrogations anymore. He asks a question. I answer. Then I ask a question and he answers."

"So change it up a bit."

"I guess I didn't have the energy. And I still haven't come up with a good response to why I haven't gotten married yet."

Grace raised her eyebrows. "He asked you that?"

"He asked me that within the first ten minutes. I was tempted to say that it's kind of hard to date in a women's prison. But seriously, he clearly wanted to know what was wrong with me. Does he think he gets points for being divorced? I could have easily gotten married and divorced too. Maybe the right answer to that question is to say that unlike many people, I had the intelligence and foresight to know when a relationship wouldn't work."

Grace laughed. "A snarky response probably wouldn't have endeared you to him. Maybe a good answer is that it just hasn't been right."

"Well most people think that if it hasn't happened by my age, then something must be wrong. I've heard it all: the ticking biological clock, statistics about the likelihood of people marrying after they pass a certain age. It's bad enough that I have to live out my life under a biological dictatorship and constant social pressure, but do I have to punch the time clock as I do it?" Mia paused and took a look at her watch while Grace waited to see if there was more to the rant. "It's after five. You probably have to get home."

"Actually, David's with the kids, so I have about an hour if you'd like to grab a drink downstairs."

"Seriously? You? Spontaneous? How about that."

"Funny," Grace said, standing and taking her jacket from the back of her chair.

◇

In the lobby bar, Mia and Grace settled into a plush red velvet booth and ordered a glass of white wine each. "So where were we?" Grace said.

"We were lamenting the tragic state of my love life, a topic of perennial interest and concern to all," Mia answered, placing her head in her hands.

"Poetic," Grace said.

But this time, Mia saw no humour in her circumstance. Typically, she would cycle from accepting and even enjoying her single status to a state of near despair. This was where she found herself today.

She and Grace had met seven years ago when Mia started working at the newspaper. They developed an intimacy rare among new friends. Together they had dissected Mia's thoughts, her fears and her behaviour, with the hope that Mia would uncover the source of her inability to connect with someone for more than five minutes. Mia had a habit of berating herself for this failure. When she showed herself more compassion, she saw that it was the result of many complex causes, some of which had nothing to do with her. But usually, she found a comfortable niche somewhere between the two extremes.

It was the not knowing that unsettled Mia. If only she knew. Would it be in two years, in five years or in ten that she was going to meet this elusive, faceless person? She would often lie awake at night doing the math: if she met him tomorrow and they dated for a year before getting married, and they wanted to be married for a while before having a family, she figured that she would be approaching her mid-forties before producing her first kid.

"Grace, you have no idea how lucky you are that you know."

"That I know what?"

"That you know that you're not going to age alone. That you have David. That you have your kids. It must be such a comfort to you."

Neither of them spoke as Grace reflected on this. Tonight Mia's ruminations were progressing well beyond the fallout of a bad date. Grace took a sip of wine, set her glass down and crossed her arms on the table.

"I do feel a sense of comfort. But the comfort, the knowing, it's all just an illusion. I can't know for sure that David and I will always be together. And who knows where my children will be in thirty or forty years when I'm older. Halfway around the world maybe. The truth is, that none of us ever really knows. This sense of permanence that you so envy doesn't exist for any of us."

"Maybe. But dismissing it as an illusion is an exaggeration. If you want to win the lottery, you have to buy a ticket. The likelihood of being surrounded by family as you get older is obviously greater if you're married now and have children."

"I get it." Grace placed her hand over Mia's. "Without giving up on getting what you want, maybe you need to rethink how you define family. Maybe it's not a husband and children. Maybe it's your sister and her kids. Maybe it's your friends. You have a rich community around you." The mention of Mia's niece and nephew brought a smile to her face. But even her niece, at eight-years-old, had wondered aloud why Mia had yet to find a man. And after Mia's last failed relationship, the little girl, woefully concerned about a life without cousins, asked Mia why she couldn't just go out and get some eggs. The misguided question both stung and amused.

◇

Mia arrived home that evening beaten. She peeled off her jacket and tossed it on the chair by the door, kicked off her shoes and let herself drop onto the couch. She shut her eyes and just listened. She was enveloped in absolute silence, interrupted briefly by the sharp honk of a car horn. Quiet was something that Mia needed, something she craved, when the clamour of traffic, the bustle of her office or the intrusive sounds from raucous neighbours persisted without reprieve. Quiet was a luxury that she enjoyed.

She tried to appreciate the moment. Even as Mia yearned for a life partner, she could also savour the sweetness of time alone with a compelling book, a good movie or her own reflections. But recounting and reliving her night out had upset her. That date was one disappointment in a string of many over the past few months.

Mia's friends had harangued her, trying to convince her to search online, until finally, with great reluctance, she entered the clandestine world of Internet dating. Her accounts of the resulting exchanges and encounters were sources of endless entertainment for those same friends, as she made efforts to remain positive and subdue the rising sense of futility. In retrospect, she should have kept her experiences to herself, but sometimes their sheer absurdity compelled her to share them. The number of dating disasters was expanding exponentially. She referenced them according to their fallout: the one where the guy asked her to lend him eight thousand dollars, the one where he forgot his wallet, the one whose posted age was a "typo."

Grace had been excited that Mia was trying something new, opening herself up to a whole new pool of prospects. She couldn't have guessed it would be a cesspool.

"Wasn't there someone recently who interested you?" she had asked.

"He was more interested in texting than actually being with me. Does he think I'm looking for a pen pal? I mean, if I wanted a relationship with my cell phone, I'd set it on vibrate and stick it in my pocket!"

They weren't all disasters, of course. There had been Will, an awkward, bespectacled biochemist, who showed up on their first date in an ill-fitting suit that Mia was sure had been purchased for his high school graduation. It wasn't just that he had followed a long line of calamities. She had truly been taken by his charm and sweetness, and by his genuine desire to get to know her. He was brilliant in a way that could have been intimidating, had he not been so unpretentious. They spent a few weeks together, enough time for Mia to begin to relax, and then Will was offered a teaching position at a university in God-Knows-Where, Oklahoma. And that was that. Will had wanted to continue seeing her, but Mia couldn't imagine a relationship with that kind of distance.

Since then, the men she met either frustrated or annoyed her. She had to fight a strong urge to run and sequester herself alone in her apartment. And yet, as she lay on her couch now, the tranquility she so desperately sought was becoming a deafening roar that mocked her.

CHAPTER 6
SARAH

Sarah picked up one of the magazines arrayed on the table in front of her. She turned the pages without reading and then closed it and tossed it back on the table. No one else was in the room though several chairs had been set out. She took in her surroundings, examining the art and assessing whether she liked it or not. A large canvas on the wall directly opposite from where she was sitting depicted a little girl on a swing. It was colourful, cheerful. But as Sarah took a closer look she noticed that the child had no facial features. It was disturbing, almost eerie. She thought about the person she was about to meet and wondered why, of all people, this would be appealing to her.

Sarah stood up, and realizing she had no place to go, sat back down and looked at her watch. When she had arrived, no one was there to greet her. She had taken a seat assuming that this is where she should be waiting. The minutes ticked by and still she was alone. Then, from somewhere down the hall, she heard the creak of a door and the clickety-clack of high heels growing louder as someone approached.

"Sarah?"

She stood and faced the woman with the extended hand.

"I'm Maggie Wallace."

"Nice to meet you, Dr. Wallace," Sarah said, surprised at the slight quiver in her voice.

"It's Maggie. Come on in."

Sarah followed her down a short hallway.

She stopped, opened the door to her office and stood aside allowing Sarah to enter before her. "Have a seat," she said.

Sarah sat down at one end of a beige upholstered sofa, assuming that the leather high back chair was Maggie's. She watched Maggie as she pulled out a pad of paper from under some books and settled into the leather chair opposite her. Sarah sized her up. Older than she was, she thought, mid- to late forties, with nondescript long, dark straight hair pulled back tightly in a ponytail. Her skin was pale and unblemished. Sarah wondered if she ever saw the sun or if her days were spent sequestered in her office listening to other people's misery. She had given little thought to her own appearance before heading out the door that morning, and now felt self-conscious in her faded jeans and loose-fitting T-shirt. She dragged her fingers through her hair, not remembering if she had run a brush through it. She glanced up at Maggie's eyes, which were hazel-coloured and warm. Maggie stood up again, stepped over to her desk and picked up the pair of glasses sitting by the phone. Maggie put them on, sat down again and faced Sarah.

"Let's just get some housekeeping out of the way," Maggie said, beginning to scribble on her pad. "Your full address is..." As Sarah gave Maggie the information, she continued to scan the room. Her eyes settled on the small antique table just beside the sofa. Beside the lamp, which provided the room with ambient lighting, was the de rigueur box of tissues. Next to the box was a clock that could easily be seen from where Maggie was sitting. Her desk, a light-coloured, distressed wood, was butted up against one wall and above it, five framed diplomas attested to Maggie's credentials. A matching armoire stood on the wall opposite Sarah. Underneath it lay an oriental carpet, which covered most of the deep brown burnished wood floor.

Maggie was mechanically jotting down Sarah's responses. Usually, Sarah either liked someone or didn't within minutes of having met them. With Maggie, Sarah was unsure. She seemed nice enough, Sarah decided, cordial, but businesslike. Maggie turned over a page and then rested the pad on her legs. Her face softened. "So, Sarah. How are you?"

"Okay, I guess." But she knew that her very presence in Maggie's office meant that she was anything but okay. Maggie didn't immediately respond, and in the void Sarah began to feel a sense of dread like she was on stage and had forgotten her lines.

"Well, let's start with why you felt you needed some help."

"It's Matthew. He's been pushing me to do this. I guess he's worried."

"And Matthew is—"

"Matthew's my husband," Sarah said, and Maggie picked up the pen and pad again to take note.

"And why is Matthew worried?"

"I haven't been out much over the past month or so since it happened." Sarah's voice broke and she bit the inside of her lip.

Maggie furrowed her brow. "You look like you want to cry," she said.

"I can't." Sarah was wringing her hands. She looked down to avoid Maggie's gaze.

"Why not?"

"For one thing, that's basically all I do. Plus, I don't even know you. I just met you. I can't just go there."

Maggie tilted her head as if in thought and waited. "A lot of people find the first session kind of awkward. It's true that we just met minutes ago and now I'm asking you to reveal the most intimate details about your life. So I get it."

Sarah squirmed. "I really don't know why I'm here to be honest. It's not like there's anything you can do. I can't have a baby. Matthew and I have been trying for what seems like forever. I get pregnant, then I lose the baby, and that's it. End of story. After that what else is there to say? And what else is there to do?" Sarah paused and looked down again. "I can't keep going through this over and over. Especially after this last time." Again, Sarah fought the tears. "There's really nothing else to say."

"How many times have you miscarried?" Maggie asked.

"Three. And then there was this last pregnancy—"

"Was there something different about this last time?"

Sarah looked at Maggie through blurred vision. "I can't." She was barely audible. "I can't." It all still seemed so unreal. She and Matthew hadn't talked much about it. Talking about it might make it more real. She didn't want to speak, but the silence between her and the therapist grew heavy. She couldn't stand the dead air.

"When Matthew and I got married, we always knew we wanted a family but we figured we'd wait a bit and have some time to ourselves, you know, just as a couple. It was always a matter of when we would have kids, not if we could. And somehow the years flew by. He and I were having so much fun just the two of us. Then finally we decided to try." Maggie nodded but said nothing.

"Anyway, I had no problem getting pregnant. The first time it happened pretty quickly and we were both so happy. Matthew told practically everyone he knew right away and I was so mad at him because I had wanted to wait. But at the same time I kind of enjoyed the excitement. Then about a month into the pregnancy..." Sarah's voice trailed off. She glanced outside. It was pouring and the raindrops were rapping against the window. She wrapped her arms around herself.

"Take your time."

"It just went away. I was upset but I was still pretty positive and I remember that at the time I was the one encouraging Matthew. I admit that it was difficult that so many people had known about the pregnancy and now had to be told that I had miscarried. And you wouldn't believe the stories that followed. At first they were helpful but at some point I couldn't bear to hear about so-and-so's sister who also miscarried the first time around and then went on to have three healthy children."

Sarah paused to allow Maggie to interject with a question or some trite comment that Sarah had become so used to hearing, but Maggie said nothing.

"None of these details are particularly important," Sarah finally said, convinced that she was boring her listener. Maggie uncrossed her legs then crossed them again and waited, still looking at Sarah.

"Don't worry about me, okay? Just say whatever comes to mind."

"Right. Okay." Sarah had never done this before and she wasn't quite sure what was expected. She pressed on, still tentative. "After the second time, I started to worry, but still, I was told that it was pretty common and not to panic. We hadn't told anyone that time. Or barely anyone. So at least it didn't happen again in front of the entire world. My parents knew. And Matthew's parents knew."

"You're shaking your head," Maggie said, though Sarah hadn't even noticed.

"I'm not sure what was harder. Losing the baby, having to tell our parents or being on the receiving end of their sympathy. And now it's so much worse. My mother. She's driving me crazy and I feel bad saying this because she is so great and so loving and I know that she only wants the best for me."

"How does she drive you crazy?"

"She treats me like I can't do anything for myself. Like I'm fragile."

"Are you?"

"Am I what?"

52

"Fragile?" Again, Sarah felt her eyes well up. The beginnings of a headache were clamouring inside her skull.

"I guess. I thought I was strong, but maybe I'm not."

"You're not strong because you're sad?"

The dam finally broke. Tears coursed down her cheeks, dropping onto her lap. She plucked a bunch of tissues from the box and dabbed at her face before looking up at Maggie.

"Sarah, what happened? You alluded to something that happened recently. What was it?"

Sarah folded the wet tissue and wrapped it around her fingers. She felt Maggie tugging at her, dragging her back to that excruciating moment that had changed everything, and she wanted to resist. *It's why I'm here. I have to go there. Trust her.*

"After the first couple of miscarriages we tried to find out what was going on. I was poked and prodded and still there was no conclusive diagnosis. I think it was the not knowing that was so difficult. If only we could have identified a cause then we would have known what we were dealing with and we could have treated it. It was all so uncertain. The doctors said 'maybe it's this' or 'maybe it's that' but no one really knew. My doctor kept reassuring me that the odds of having a successful pregnancy after several losses were in my favour, but statistics didn't really mean a hell of a whole lot to me." Her voice was much stronger now.

"You sound angry."

"I am angry," she said, more loudly than she'd meant to. "But the sadness usually eclipses that." Sarah fell silent.

"I'm sorry, Sarah. I interrupted you. Please continue."

"My doctor couldn't find anything that could medically explain why this kept happening. He even suggested that my problems might be stress-related. As if I brought it on myself."

"When physical explanations elude them, some doctors toss the issues into the psychology basket," Maggie said. "But I'm more interested in what you thought."

"I don't know. I'm not a doctor. But I can tell you that for the first two pregnancies I really don't remember feeling stressed. Even after the first miscarriage, even though I was devastated, I still don't think I was particularly anxious the second time. For the third and fourth pregnancies, I guess there was a lot of apprehension despite my best efforts." Sarah choked back a sob and covered her face with her hands. "What did I do wrong?"

"You think that you somehow caused your miscarriages?"

"I told you. I don't know." Sarah grabbed another tissue and hid her face. Maggie waited. "Even if it wasn't stress, obviously there is something wrong with my body, isn't there?" She looked at Maggie who was considering the question.

"So you do blame yourself. If not for something you did, then for something you are?"

Sarah didn't answer. She was exhausted and had no idea where any of this was going. "Matthew started talking about other options, but I couldn't think about the possibility of not having my own child. And then..." Sarah stopped.

"Then?"

"Then finally. Finally, when I got pregnant for the fourth time I managed to hold on to the baby after the first three months. And then four months, then five and six months, and I was feeling great and doing great." And with that, Sarah recounted the events of that day when she had, without warning, been hurled off course.

◇

It was a Tuesday and Matthew was at work. Sarah had decided to take the day off and was at home, sitting in the living room chair with her nose buried in a book and Lucy at her feet. She idly rubbed her expanding belly and was hard-pressed to imagine that it could grow any more. Now seven and a half months pregnant, Sarah had gained thirty pounds. She was feeling tired and sluggish but also euphoric. Perhaps the only person on the planet who was happier than she, was Matthew, who spent much of his time either caressing Sarah's stomach or speaking to her belly button. Sarah's friends had often complained about the sense of entitlement of strangers, who apparently thought that a pregnant woman's body became public property and was available to all for groping. Sarah, on the other hand, felt a rush of excitement whenever someone in an elevator or at the supermarket reached out to pat her belly, or to ask whether she was having a boy or a girl. Any affirmation of her condition was sheer bliss.

But on this Tuesday, something was off. With her hand still on her stomach, she looked up from her book and frowned. She rose from the chair and lay down on her side on the couch. The night before, as she and Matthew were getting into bed, Sarah had mentioned that Ben was kind of quiet. But Matthew wasn't alarmed, nor did he sense Sarah's real concern. "Enjoy it," he had said. "Soon you won't be getting any quiet at all."

But now the eerie stillness within her persisted. She sat up to reach for the phone and dialled. As she listened to the pre-recorded message telling her to wait on the line, she realized she was perspiring. She got up and paced the living room with Lucy trailing at her feet. She felt lightheaded and for a moment feared she might pass out. Sarah sat back down and put her hand on her chest, feeling the beat of her heart.

"Dr. Kerr's office."

"Hello, this is Sarah Hoffman. I'm probably overreacting but I haven't felt the baby move in quite some time. Is this normal?"

"One moment please."

Sarah got up again and moved to the kitchen. She sat down at the table and glanced up at the clock over the door. The second hand moved around the clock. Tick, tick, tick. Then again. She heard a beep. Call waiting. Sarah pulled the phone from her ear to look at the call display. Matthew. She ignored him. Then seconds later, her cell phone rang. Sarah stood and went over to her purse on the kitchen counter. Still holding the phone to her ear with one hand, she rummaged through her bag in search of her cell.

"Hello?"

"Hey."

"Matthew, I'm on hold with the doctor's office."

"What's going on?"

"I still haven't felt the baby move." She paused. "I'm worried."

He was quiet for a moment and then said, "I'm sure there's nothing to worry about, Sarah. But I guess it's a good idea to—" Sarah missed the end of his sentence when the receptionist came back on the line.

"Ms. Hoffman?"

"Yes?"

"Could you come in now?"

"Now?"

"Yes. Now. Dr. Kerr can see you." Brusque, to the point, cold.

"I'm on my way." She hung up the phone, forgetting that she still had Matthew on the line.

"Sarah? Sarah, are you still there?"

"I'm going in. Can you meet me?"

Silence on the other end.

"Matthew!"

"I'll meet you." And they hung up.

Sarah arrived first and was in the examination room waiting for the doctor when Matthew came into the room. They looked at one another, seeing the reflection of their own fears in each other's eyes. Matthew took Sarah's hand and kissed it. Then the doctor entered.

"Hello, Sarah." He acknowledged Matthew with a nod of the head. "So how long has it been since you've felt any fetal movement?"

Dr. Kerr adjusted the earpieces of his stethoscope and placed the flat disk of the chest piece on Sarah's stomach.

"Some time yesterday afternoon I think."

Dr. Kerr frowned and moved the stethoscope. Both Sarah and Matthew studied his face, but his expression was inscrutable. "Let's do an ultrasound," he said, wheeling the equipment to the examining table.

"Is something wrong?" Matthew squeezed her hand, watching as Dr. Kerr squirted gel onto Sarah's skin.

Dr. Kerr glided the probe over Sarah's belly and she no longer had to look to him for signs. The glorious swishing of her baby's heartbeat had been replaced with a vacuous empty space.

◇

Sarah was crying now. The intensity, the raw explosive pain that had detonated within her just over one month ago now returned.

"I'm so sorry, Sarah," Maggie said.

"I had to give birth to him, you know. I had to give birth to a dead boy." Sarah paused, still unable to absorb the enormity of that day. "What was supposed to be a moment of joy..." Sarah didn't finish the thought. "It's so ironic."

"What is?" Maggie asked.

"What happened was completely random. It had nothing to do with the problems I had before then. A knot in the umbilical cord cut off the baby's blood supply." A gasp escaped from Maggie's mouth. "I didn't even know what that was, that it could even happen. My doctor kept saying, 'The important thing, Sarah, is that you almost went full term. That's good news.' I could have killed him. I really couldn't find good news in any of this. But one thing is clear. I was not meant to have a baby."

"You believe that?"

"I don't know. What I do know is that I can't go through this again. I'm done."

"Sarah, you're mourning the loss of your child. Your heart is broken. Allow yourself some time to heal."

Maggie was right of course, Sarah thought. But healing from a wound so deep was not something that she could imagine at this moment.

CHAPTER 7

KATE

Kate lay motionless. The feeling of the cool bathroom floor against her left cheek was soothing. She had spent the better part of the morning trying to eat a piece of dry toast, and had used her last bit of energy regurgitating it. A drop of perspiration inched its way down from her hairline and burned as it reached her eye. She blinked it away and ran a hand across her face. Her skin was clammy. She reached beside her for the robe that she had torn off her body as she heaved into the toilet. As she draped it over herself, there was a light tap on the door. "Kate? You okay?" The question, like the answer, was absurd.

"Fine, Daniel."

"Do you need anything?"

"No."

What she needed was to escape her body. Kate's mind was drawn back to the very first day she was introduced to the nurse who had been assigned to her. By the time she had arrived at the hospital for her second treatment three weeks earlier, her resolve was weakening. The fortress of strength was crumbling already. *I'm fine, I'm managing.* That had been her stock response. But the fallout of the first treatment had been so unrelenting, so cruel, that walking voluntarily into the hospital for the second round was unthinkable. Knowing that

Angel would be right beside her was the only thing that got her there. Angel, nicknamed by another grateful patient, had extended her hand and supported Kate through the pain.

Now, as Kate lay on the bathroom floor, she heard Angel's voice, calm and tender, telling her to visualize her suffering and then imagine letting it go. Kate had initially laughed at the suggestion, but Angel insisted that it had brought many patients relief. Whether it was her belief in Angel or out of sheer desperation, Kate closed her eyes, wrapped the robe tightly around herself and mentally drew the object of her torment.

The nausea, intense as it was, emerged as a translucent, amorphous green blob, swelling like a jellyfish as it swam. Tentacles extended outward from the mass, growing larger and flailing wildly. The vision expanded slowly, bulging and then contracting. As if taking a breath, it bulged and contracted again. The blackness behind the green mass began to lighten, first to gray, then a hazy blue. The colour intensified and sharpened until it looked like a summer sky. In the distance, Kate saw the outline of a bird with a large wingspan gliding through the air, descending as it grew closer. Hovering just inches over the ground and without slowing, it snatched up the green mass, lifted and soared.

Kate opened her eyes and sat up. She felt calmer, but the nausea had not subsided and her head was now beginning to throb. She grabbed onto the edge of the vanity and hoisted herself up to a standing position. The room started to spin. When she was certain that she was stable she opened her eyes, turned on the faucet and splashed cold water on her face. In the mirror, distress lines were forming on the bridge of her nose between her eyebrows. Her face was gaunt and pale.

When she shuffled out of the bathroom, Daniel was sitting on the bed reading the paper. "You're still here," she said. It was more of a statement than a question.

"I'm just leaving." He jumped up from the bed as if he had been on his way out.

"I think I finally understand the reason for this kind of suffering," she said, moving towards the vacated mattress. "Death starts to look pretty good."

He ignored her morbid attempt at humour. "I thought they gave you something for the nausea."

"Yeah, well, I guess it didn't work. Do you have many appointments today?" she asked, trying to divert the conversation.

"A few. There's been quite a bit of interest in the Benson house lately."

"Finally. I was beginning to lose hope on that one," Kate said. She paused. "I really miss that rush. The back and forth, the offers and counter offers. The thrill of closing a deal."

"You can come back anytime you want, you know," Daniel said.

"It's really not the type of thing I can just breeze in and out of," she snapped. "You have to be available at all kinds of hours, and I don't think our clients would appreciate my puking in the bathroom that I'm trying to sell them."

"Whatever you want," he said with a sigh. "I'll see you at dinner."

"See you later." Kate felt guilty about being impatient with her husband, something that was happening with increasing frequency. He was trying to help, but he just didn't know how. She wished that she could tell him how he could help. But she didn't know either. Not that they ever talked about it, mind you. Not once did they look each other square in the eye and say they were scared. It was the pragmatist in her. Somehow she, and by extension they, had leapt directly into the business of fighting this thing without any real acknowledgement that she could die. That this disease could kill her.

Kate lay down and massaged her forehead, trying to ease the pain that had begun to intensify. Angel had told her that she would feel fatigued much of the time but that too much rest could make her even more tired. Too little rest wasn't good either, she had said. Kate had looked at her, bemused.

As she lay on the bed trying to muster the strength to get up, Kate's mind turned back to Daniel. She imagined him meeting his clients – their clients, really – engaging them, and invariably earning their trust. He had that quality.

◇

When Kate first met Daniel almost thirty years ago, it was the first thing she had noticed. They were standing in the empty space that would eventually become her home. It was the ground floor of a triplex and Kate could picture herself living there from the moment she walked in and saw the exposed brick in the living room. Daniel had taken the time to understand what her needs were, showed her places within her budget and was not overly pushy. That her agent would move in, one year later, to the very house he had sold her, was not something that Kate could have predicted.

Kate had been in her mid-twenties and aimless. She had graduated a few years earlier, fallen backwards into an unfulfilling, average-paying job because her father knew someone who knew someone, and was biding her time until she could find her calling. While most of her friends were on well-defined paths, building careers, Kate had been slower to evolve. It drove her father crazy. Her mother, more patient by nature, knew that Kate would find her way in her own time and on her own terms. Despite her lack of direction, Kate had the foresight to know that regardless of what lay ahead, investing in real estate would pay off. What she didn't foresee was that it would yield much more than financial dividends.

Daniel had waited until Kate signed on the dotted line, but not one second longer. When he suggested that they celebrate her new home with a drink together she was surprised by the invitation. Not once throughout their professional dealings had he ever intimated that there might be personal interest.

"So how long have you been working in real estate?" she asked that evening over dinner.

"I guess it's about four years now."

"You were licensed after university?"

"No. When I graduated I had no idea what I wanted to do. So I bummed around Europe for about six months which thrilled my parents to no end." Kate thought of her own dad and laughed. "It's a little embarrassing to admit, but when I came back my only preoccupation was making money. I knew that I had the personality for selling and the real estate course was relatively short. I know, not the most noble of ambitions," Daniel said. "And I have to say I was a bit deluded when I first got started. It can be lucrative but you really have to establish yourself and that takes time. But since I've been in it, I've actually really grown to love it for reasons that I would never have anticipated."

"Such as?"

"This may sound corny but I feel like I'm helping people to realize a dream."

"I never thought of it that way," Kate said.

"Neither had I. But take yourself for example. You just bought your first home. It's more than just a house to you isn't it?"

"I suppose it is. It's an achievement." The flame in Daniel's eyes was infectious and Kate felt a flood of exhilaration that went far beyond the excitement of her purchase. Until then, Kate had been as non-committal in her love life as she had been in her professional life. She had dated some, but wasn't even sure that she wanted to get married or have children, though she would admit only to herself that

63

this was more of a rebellion against expectation than a true wish.

Now, sitting before her, was a man who was making her wonder what their kids might be like. Daniel was unlike the skinny, lanky men she usually went for. He was tall, lean and toned. She preferred a clean-shaven face, but Daniel's auburn, neatly trimmed goatee was sexy. She felt her face grow warm as she imagined what he might look like under his clothes. Kate was also tall, just a couple of inches shorter than Daniel, and had chestnut-coloured hair and blue eyes. She hated her aquiline nose, always had, and never believed her mother when she said it gave her character. That night, with Daniel, she couldn't help but think that she might have hit the genetic jackpot.

Still unable to move from her bed, she thought about her three teenage kids. Seth was tall but had gotten her nose, though he didn't seem to notice. On him, Kate really did believe that it added character. Seventeen-year-old Michael was the same height as his fifteen-year-old sister, which he did not appreciate. Kate was never able to see any part of herself or Daniel in Michael. And neither could he. He was so different in looks and personality that when he was a child Kate had to repeatedly convince him that he was not adopted. And then there was Zoë, who seemed to have gotten the best of both of them with her azure eyes, flaxen hair and a lean frame that seemed to be drawing a lot of male attention lately. And her nose was perfect. More importantly for Kate, Zoë had turned out to be an exceptional young woman. She was genuine and kind. She was feisty, like Kate, and driven. Yes, Zoë had gotten the best parts of Kate. What remained to be seen was whether Zoë would inherit the very worst of her too. That Zoë might one day have to face the same physical devastation was Kate's greatest fear. But she kept this fear to herself, because Daniel would not be able to handle it and Zoë should not have to.

CHAPTER 8
SOPHIE

When Sophie was introduced to Alex Bauman by her mother's cousin, she tried to keep an open mind. They were a perfect match on paper, the cousin had said, so hopes were high that they would be perfect in life. When she continued to date Alex it was to mollify her father, who, although Sophie was only twenty-three, was bluntly inquiring about her dating activity. Despite this apparent interest, he usually greeted the men she brought home with little more than a disdainful glance.

Though they never spoke of it, she and her dad both missed her mother. In the last months of her mother's life, as Sophie was starting university, Sophie had watched her mother transform into an unrecognizable version of herself. Sophie had never experienced such intense and sustained pain. It had taken two years, but the pain did subside. Her father, on the other hand, was in a perpetual state of anger, acrimony dripping from his every word. "Wretched cancer," he would say at any opportunity. But when she introduced her father to Alex, she saw him soften, and Sophie caught a glimpse of the person who had existed before her mother died.

When she agreed to marry Alex eighteen months after first meeting him, it was to end the barrage of proposals which, until then, she had flatly declined. She felt she and Alex were too young to get married and she wanted to finish school.

"What difference does it make whether or not we've finished school?" he had asked, frustration mounting every time she raised the issue.

"I don't know. We should be settled, with jobs, in a place of our own."

"But why *should* we?" When he whined, Sophie lost patience.

"Because, Alex, it's irresponsible."

"Irresponsible? Money isn't a problem, Soph. You know that. We're going to get married *someday,* so why not now? Besides which, you hate law school. Why are you so hell bent on finishing?"

She did hate law school. But her father was right. What would she do with a fine arts degree? And Alex was right. Sophie also thought that they would eventually get married. He loved her. That she knew. And that, she believed, should be enough. Plus, it would make her dad happy.

As she thought back to those many conversations, she realized that she and Alex had never talked about what marriage meant. They had never had a forthright exchange about what each of them wanted, not only from each other, but also in life. Somewhere along the way, Sophie had become a cookie-cutter wife and mother, and Alex was the patriarch who justified his long work hours with excuses of having a family to support. So it was not unusual that he had to be in court on the day the kids were heading off to camp leaving Sophie to say all the goodbyes.

Standing in the parking lot, she relinquished her hold on Gabe only after he said he couldn't breathe, and she kissed Jessie's face and cupped it in her hands for a few moments longer than Jessie was comfortable.

"C'mon, Mom, I better go."

"I'm going to miss you so much, Jess."

"I'll miss you too, but geez, it's just for a month."

"I know. Be good. Take care of Gabe and write to me a lot, okay?

"Sure." Jessie gave her mother one last peck on the cheek and, taking her brother's hand, trotted off toward the bus. Sophie waited until the kids boarded and stayed in the parking lot until the moment the bus drove off, waving frantically, though she couldn't see either of her kids.

When she got home, she dropped onto the sofa and draped her arm over her eyes so that she wouldn't see the cyclonic disaster that was her living room. Sophie could never quite figure out how she and Lydia could be so organized and yet, on the day that the kids left for camp, there was always a frantic rush with all sorts of last minute things to do. The bags were packed the night before with the camp lists duly checked off, but invariably Gabe would have to find a video game, Jessie would insist on emptying her closet to ensure that nothing critical was left behind, and the trunks and duffels would be reopened, resulting in a holy mess.

Sophie adored her children. Sometimes she thought that she adored them too much, if that were possible. When Jessie was born, Sophie used to hover over her crib for hours, watching her tiny chest rise and fall. If there was even a brief break in her breaths, Sophie panicked. Her friends admitted they did the same thing, so Sophie resented Alex's teasing. One evening, when Alex told Sophie about a dinner invitation from one of the firm's partners, he took it for granted that she'd join him.

"I'm not ready to leave Jessie," she had said. "She's four months old."

"We're not abandoning her, Sophie," Alex said, derision oozing from every word. "There'll be a babysitter."

"I'm not leaving her with a babysitter!" Even she could acknowledge that she was being irrational, reacting as if Alex had suggested something akin to criminal negligence. "I'm really sorry," she said, feeling some remorse but still unable to yield to his persuasion.

"Maybe your mother could come," he suggested.

"I can't go. You'll be fine without me."

"Look, this dinner is kind of a big deal. I haven't been work-ing at this firm for that long and I need to make a place for myself. You know, get in with the partners."

"Sorry, Alex."

His ears turned crimson and his dark eyes narrowed. "You can't be serious! It's as if no one else matters. Jessie's the only one who can get your attention. What about what I need?"

"This isn't about you."

"It is about me. I'm your husband, not just your kid's father."

"I'm not going."

On the evening of the Saturday dinner, Sophie could see that Alex was still hoping she would change her mind. He passed silently by Jessie's bedroom where she was cradling their daughter in her arms and rocking her in the chair by her crib. For the two weeks since they had argued about this evening, Alex had stayed late at work, wordlessly punishing her for her choice.

Her friends were more understanding. They said that her postpartum obsessiveness was normal and that it would eventually wane. Soon, they told her, she would be yearning for an evening out, for conversation that was more stimulating than the unintelligible exchanges she had with her daughter, for an uninterrupted dinner with her husband. But that didn't happen. Sophie never craved any of those things. She could stay in day after day, night after night, without needing a reprieve from Jessie. When she did venture out, it was more from a sense of obligation to Alex or her friends than for pleasure. When she was away from home, she would wait until an appropriate amount of time had elapsed and then suggest to whomever she was with that they should call it a night.

Sophie was so devoted to Jessie that despite Alex's urgings, she put off having another child out of fear that her attention would be divided. Alex was dying to have more children and when Sophie finally agreed, it was to placate him and assuage her guilt for neglecting him. When Gabe was born, she and Alex were both elated and what she thought had been her motivation seemed absurd.

By that time, Jessie was five and had started kindergarten, so Gabe filled the empty space created by her absence. Jessie was in awe of her brother and when she got home from school she doted on him. Both she and Sophie did this together so Sophie never felt she was dividing her attention between her children. When Alex would arrive home, he'd caress Jessie's cheek, ask her the customary questions about school, scoop up Gabe in his arms and kiss his wife. Picture perfect.

Sophie thought about the long, empty month that stretched out before her now that her kids were in camp. She got up from the couch, went into the den and sat down at the antique desk. It felt a little strange taking pen to paper when she and her kids were so used to communicating via phone, email and texts.

> *Dear Jessie,*
> *I dropped you off at the bus barely an hour ago and already I'm counting the days until you and Gabe are home. Life isn't the same without the two of you around. I am sure by the time you get this letter you will be settled in and enjoying your days at camp. I am anxious to hear about your counsellors and bunkmates and all the fun that you are having. I will check out the camp website every day to take a look at the photos that are posted and will be looking for Gabe's and your smiling faces. Remember to wear sunscreen and swim with a buddy. What can I say? I'm your mother. I worry. I can't wait for our trip to Maine next month. Write soon. Love, Mom.*

Sophie reread the letter once, placed it in the envelope and sealed it. She took out another piece of paper and wrote a similar note to Gabe. Pulling a stack of stamps from the desk drawer she applied one to each letter and, with letters in hand, she headed out the door and walked up to the corner to drop them in the mailbox. When she got home, she flung her purse on the chair in the hallway, went back into the living room and glanced at her watch. Thirty minutes had passed. It would still be hours until dinnertime and she was tired of shopping to fill the gaps between mealtimes. There were no errands to run for the kids and she did not have to pick them up from anywhere.

As if by some wave of a wand the room was no longer a mess. She silently thanked Lydia, who had obviously tackled it while Sophie was writing her letters and running to the mailbox. It seemed indulgent to have someone clean up after her family when she could easily do it. She had the time, after all. With hands on hips, Sophie scanned the room and thought about what she might do next.

"Is this it? Is this all there is? It can't be," she said to the walls. "It can't be," she said again, punctuating every word, her voice escalating. "It can't be," she repeated, her breath turning short and ragged. "It can't be! It can't be!" She was yelling now and weeping. Sophie collapsed onto the sofa, grabbed a pillow and buried her face in it.

Kate. The thought of her friend brought a feeling of shame. "I don't have the right to want more," Sophie said, aloud. "I have so much. Kate has a right to be angry. To be frustrated. To be unhappy. To be scared. I have no right. I have no right." But she could not talk herself out of the desolation.

CHAPTER 9

MIA

Mia could not still her mind. She tried to focus on her breath as instructed. Inhale. Exhale.

During the hour and a half that she spent twice weekly in her yoga class, Mia was usually able to centre herself and revitalize her mind and body, no matter what had come before or what was waiting for her after class. But today she couldn't relax. She lost her balance and stumbled out of tree pose.

"If you fall, show yourself some compassion and just try again," the instructor said. Mia inhaled, shifted her weight over her left foot and drew the sole of her right foot up to her inner thigh. She brought the palms of her hands together in front of her chest and softened her gaze. Still, she could not quiet the clamour in her head and stop thinking about the interview she'd had earlier in the day.

Mia was used to the health beat, covering stories that were sad or tragic. She loved her job because oftentimes those same stories were potent sources of inspiration. Her fascination with anything medical helped her to absorb the information that she gathered when interviewing doctors about scientific discoveries, medical miracles and, in this case, their high costs. She had already met with Andrew Patton's physician about his liver transplant, and that morning she'd visited Andrew in his home.

◇

Mia hadn't known what to expect. She rang the doorbell and waited, but there was no movement inside the small house. She rang again. Mia heard a man's voice, an unintelligible bellow, and then the sound of footsteps. A woman, whom Mia assumed was Andrew's wife, let her in and ushered her into the living room where Andrew was lying fully dressed on the sofa. His wife offered her a drink, which Mia declined, and then retreated to the kitchen barely looking in the direction of her husband. "Come on in, Mia. Have a seat," Andrew Patton said, gesturing at the one armchair in the room.

"Thanks for taking the time to meet with me," she said, and without bothering to engage in small talk, launched into a series of questions. She asked him about his illness, his recovery period, the likelihood of rejection and resuming regular activities. Andrew related some of what she already knew. He had advanced cirrhosis, the cause of which he flippantly attributed to having had a few too many martinis. And he was fortunate in that he had a shorter wait given that he received the liver from a living donor, his brother.

"The five-year survival rate for liver transplants using living donors is about 78%," he said, "so I have every reason to be optimistic." Andrew's doctor had given her this same statistic and she was struck then, as she was now, by the reference to a living donor. The surgery had been just six weeks earlier and Andrew figured it would be another few months before he went back to work. He answered her questions succinctly and offered no elaboration. "Other than being plied with every possible medication," he said, "I suppose I have nothing to complain about." And then, as if wanting to change the focus of the interview, he said something else. "My physical recovery's not such a big deal. It'll take time, that's all. The other stuff is way heavier. I have no idea how I'm going to get past it."

Mia knew exactly what he was referring to. It was why she had come to his home. There was a sad irony to the circumstances of the transplant, and she knew that it would fascinate readers. She had thought Andrew Patton would be reluctant to talk about his brother, but found that he was willing, even grateful, to articulate thoughts and feelings probably few dared to ask him about. Mia glanced down at the list of questions that she prepared but Andrew didn't wait for them.

"I am having a hard time reconciling my survival with its cost. Greg and I were aware of the risks but somehow the potential benefit seemed to outweigh the possibility that something might happen to him. At least it did for me. And now I think I was selfish. I so wanted him to do this. I was so desperate. My life depended on this transplant."

"I understand that the doctors don't know what went wrong," Mia interjected.

Andrew was shaking his head. "No, we're not sure. He went into cardiac arrest. But why did that happen? They can't say."

"Were you and Greg close?"

"No, not really," Andrew said. "Most people assume we were. A gesture like that would have to come out of a loving, respectful relationship between brothers, you would think. Greg and I were competitive. He had all the things that I wanted. A great job, money, a beautiful wife, two daughters." Andrew glanced in the direction of the kitchen and sighed. "As a writer, I've done all right, but I'll never make my millions. Everything seemed to come so much easier to him. He never had to struggle. And then I got sick. Things got tough. But Greg and I don't live in the same city. Didn't live in the same city. So he never really knew the extent of my problems and I didn't want him to know. Pride, I guess."

"Yet, you were able to ask him for help when things got really bad."

"I had no choice. There was no one else to ask. And what killed me is that he didn't even hesitate. He agreed right away, without thinking twice about it."

"Why did that kill you?"

"Because I felt so guilty. I had always resented him. Now here he was doing this unbelievable thing for me." Andrew paused for a moment. "You know, for the life of me, I can't remember if I thanked him."

"You seem to have gained perspective."

"I have a lot of time on my hands. All I do is lie around, so there's a lot of time to obsess about things that I can't change." Andrew stopped and smiled. "But yes, on the positive side, I suppose I have fresh insights into my relationship with Greg."

The people Mia interviewed frequently divulged their thoughts and feelings. Once she had someone sitting in front of her, she could usually get what she needed and sometimes more. Mia had a manner that encouraged trust and it had served her well. People she interviewed often became emotional, and when she returned to her office, Grace would ask if she gave them the Barbara Walters treatment.

"How is your brother's family dealing with the situation?"

"They're devastated. I would've thought that they would hate me. But just like Greg, they believe that he did what he had to do and the outcome was nobody's fault. I took their husband and father from them. I don't know how I can ever make it up."

"I don't know that you ever could, but maybe you can build with them the kind of relationship you wished you had with Greg," Mia said, feeling more like a shrink than a journalist. She started to think that she had ventured too far, but there was something completely engrossing about the story that was unfolding before her.

"Well, that's exactly it. That was my conclusion too. I will do everything I can to try and fill the gap that has been left by my brother's death and be present for them, as a brother-in-law and an uncle. If they want that." Andrew looked down and rubbed the face of his watch with his thumb, shaking his head. "His wife gave this to me. She said Greg would have wanted me to have something of his." Andrew looked up at Mia. "I tried to accept it with grace but all I could feel was shame. I mean, I already have something of his."

Mia looked down at her notes and her questions but Andrew continued talking.

"I'm happy to have it," he said, fiddling with the watch band. "This might sound strange, but when I wear it, somehow I feel like he's with me and that I can be as strong as he was. I don't know, I can't explain it. It took this experience to love him, but now that I do, it's like I'm absorbing some of him through this watch." Andrew threw back his head and laughed. "That sounds so hocus-pocus, I know."

Mia was clutching the crystal hanging around her neck. "It doesn't sound strange at all," she said. "I'm pretty sure I have everything I need. Would you mind if I called you if I have more questions?"

"Not at all."

Only as Mia was leaving did she take note of the knot that had formed in her stomach, a feeling that stayed with her for the rest of the day.

Even yoga class could not release it. The pain of Andrew's story was unnerving, but the story of the brothers really got to her. There was no way for them to fix their relationship. She thought of her own dealings with her sister. They got along well. She imagined for a moment a future without marriage, and remembered Grace's comment about how we define family. Even if she never found a husband or bore children, she would still have a family. Would that be enough? She wasn't sure.

Mia suspected Andrew's marriage was something short of blissful. But really, she had no idea. She didn't know these people and the distance she'd perceived between them earlier that day might have been due to a spat before she arrived. Who knew? Regardless. Too many people got it wrong when they married. It was consoling to think that these people were no more successful than she was. And Andrew was feeling a kind of regret that she would never face, because she nurtured her family members and her friends.

These thoughts finally calmed Mia. She was seated with her legs crossed and hands pressed together over her chest. She listened to the deep *Om* reverberate through the room and her eyes welled. "*Namaste,*" she said, and bowed to the teacher and to the other students in the room.

"Wow, that was more of a challenge than I thought it would be," Mia heard someone say. She began rolling up her mat unaware that the comment was directed at her. When she glanced up, a man she hadn't noticed was looking at her, waiting.

"Oh. Yes. Pretty challenging, huh?" Mia had stopped looking for interesting guys at yoga class a long time ago, primarily because there never were any. Now, standing before her, was someone she had never seen before. His sweaty T-shirt was evidence of his claim that the class had been a challenge. He was in shape, she noticed, taller than her by a few inches and he was smiling. Mia figured he was in his mid-thirties. "Is this your first time taking a yoga class?"

"Yup. Anyone who says that yoga is just a bunch of stretches hasn't tried it, that's for sure."

"I had the same reaction the first time I tried it. You'd be surprised how addictive it can become. I hate to miss a class."

"Good to know," he said. "I'm Robert."

CHAPTER 10
SARAH

"We're going out," Emma announced when Sarah opened the door to her sister.

"We are? I don't feel like it."

"It's too beautiful a day to spend in your house. Let's go for a walk. You'll feel better."

"A walk outside will make everything better? You're not telling me to buck up, are you?" Sarah was angry, but she retreated when she remembered to whom she was speaking. "Sorry, Em."

Sarah didn't think beauty of any kind would ever reach her again, but now that she was out, the warm summer air on her skin felt good. Emma slipped her arm through Sarah's and drew her sister in close. The two walked side-by-side, the silence between them occasionally broken by a call if Lucy trotted too far in front of them. Lucy would run back, look at Sarah in pure happiness and excitement, and then take off again.

"I saw a therapist the other day," Sarah said.

"Really? Was it helpful?"

"I don't know. Maybe. I guess so. It was only one time. I'm going back again, so we'll see." They fell back into silence. Sarah was relieved that Emma didn't ask what the therapist had said. Matthew had, and when she tried to recount some of what had taken place during the session, it seemed to dilute and diminish the experience. Sarah was unable to say which of Maggie's words were helpful, nor could she say that she felt better after the session. What she had felt was relief. Relief that she could unburden herself without having to be concerned about the impact on her listener. Without having to see the pain in Matthew's eyes, or the worry on her mother's face.

Sarah and Emma walked into the small park down the street from Sarah's house. Lucy circled a tree and pawed at a paper cup. When she was bored with that, she sprinted toward Emma and Sarah before noticing a stick in her path, which she immediately picked up in her mouth and then strutted regally through the park. She dropped the stick to sniff the grass and sneezed.

"The joy of dogs. They really don't need much to be happy, do they?" Sarah asked.

"We could learn from them," Emma said, sitting down on a bench. Sarah sat down beside her and they watched Lucy, whose attention had been caught by a miniature poodle. Lucy bounded up to it and stood over the tiny creature, which lifted its nose to meet Lucy's.

"Come, Lucy!" Sarah shouted. Lucy glanced up to acknowledge Sarah's command, but then returned to her newfound friend. "Lucy!" Lucy dashed back to Sarah and Emma and placed her front paws on the bench, coming face to face with Sarah. Sarah rubbed her neck and then nudged her paws gently down to the ground. Lucy looked at Sarah, then at Emma, and finally lay down at their feet.

"So how's life, Em? Or should I say, Dr. Hoffman?" It was a challenge for Sarah to shift the focus from what constantly occupied her mind, but she recognized that her situation had completely eclipsed this achievement in Emma's life. Something else to feel guilty about. What was worse, their mother had been concentrating on Sarah to the exclusion of her other daughter, something they had both noticed.

Emma was modest, as always. "Not quite yet."

"But soon, Emma. Really soon!"

"I know. It's so hard to believe. I'm pretty excited but it is kind of scary. If I make a mistake it could have serious consequences."

Sarah nodded. "I know. But what an achievement. I'm so proud of you. I haven't said it lately, but I am."

"Thanks. I know you are but it's nice to hear every now and again."

Sarah caught the subtext. "I guess we've all been a bit preoccupied. Mom and Dad have been focussing all their attention on me. Especially Mom. It's not fair and I'm sorry."

"That's how it should be, Sarah."

"You don't always have to be so selfless, Emma. Besides which, all this attention, having my every move scrutinized, it's suffocating. I can't live under all these watchful eyes. I just need to be, without having to answer questions about how I'm feeling, or what I'm thinking, or whether or not I want to consider other options, or when I'm going back to work. I'm not there yet. I can still feel the weight of him in my arms. I can still see his beautiful little face. Hear the thud of earth as it dropped onto his tiny coffin."

Emma winced. "How's..." Emma started and then stopped herself.

"It's okay. Questions from you are somehow less annoying."

"Oh, great. Less annoying is not quite what I was striving for." They both laughed, appreciative of the moment.

"How's Matthew doing?" Emma asked, completing her thought.

"Matthew tries to put on a brave face for me. But he's suffering. Neither of us knows what to do for the other."

"I think you said it, Sarah. You just have to be. Just live it, together, with all that it entails."

"The thing is, though, we're both hurting, but we're not in

the same place. He seems to think that the best way to get over this is to move forward. Last night he said, 'It's like we've fallen into an abyss. If we have a plan, if we look toward the future, we'll get out quicker.'"

"You don't feel the same way?"

"We are in a hole, that's for damn sure. A deep one." Sarah felt the tears coming and paused, something she did routinely to stop them. "But what nobody seems to understand is that I'm not ready to be lifted out. I want to stay here for a while. I owe it to Ben."

"And here we are doing everything we possibly can to help you get over this instead of helping you through it. Maybe you just need someone to sit with you, wherever you happen to be."

Sarah felt a sudden surge of love for her sister. They had always understood each other. "Matthew's not one to sit around. He has always been the problem solver."

"But does he get it? When you explain how you're feeling and what you need right now?"

"He says he does. But then he'll come out with these statements like he did last night."

"What does he mean when he talks about a plan, anyway?"

"He wants us to decide what to do next. Do we try again? Do we start thinking about other possibilities?"

"How can I help? Tell me what I can do."

"I'm not sure," Sarah said as she gave her sister's question some thought.

Emma made a face. She had an inordinate amount of patience, but she liked people to be direct. "Just say it, Sarah. I'm asking."

"I need you to let me talk about him."

"About the baby?"

"Yes, about Ben. You can't feel connected to him in the same way that I do, but bear with me. I bonded with him. I saw him, I held him. To most people he barely existed because he didn't even take one breath in this world. But he was a person. He was my son and though I didn't get to know him well, or see him grow, I loved him."

Whenever Sarah mentioned Ben's name to her parents, friends, or even to Matthew, they tried to change the topic. The need to give her son life persisted, and she was frustrated by these misguided efforts to protect her.

"It's so obvious. How did I miss that?" Emma asked, though Sarah did not think the question was directed at her. "Of course you want to talk about him. When anyone dies we take the time to talk about them and remember them. I guess this is really no different, is it?" Emma appeared confused as she tried to work out her thoughts aloud. "Except that we don't have any memories of him."

"No, we don't. But for me, Ben is not just that baby that I cradled in my arms for a few fleeting moments. He is a little boy who will never learn to walk, or talk or ride a bike. He is a teenager who will not have noble ideals and make plans to save the world. A young man who will never graduate from high school or university. He will never be a husband or father. He will not become an inspiring teacher or a gifted artist or a brilliant doctor like his aunt. He will not share inside jokes with his father or be eternally protective of his mother. That is what we have lost."

Sarah looked at her sister, whose face was now streaming with tears. Emma took Sarah's hands. "I'm so sorry, Sarah. I'm so sorry. I didn't know." Sarah put her arms around Emma feeling her body quake with the grief over her sister's loss and the loss of her own nephew.

CHAPTER II

MIA

Mia glanced sideways at Robert as the lights came up in the theatre. He was applauding, though Mia could not tell if it was genuine enthusiasm or forced courtesy. Though they had discovered many shared interests in the first weeks of dating, theatre had not been one of them, so Mia had been surprised when he suggested they see a play together.

As the audience members began to rise and make their way to the exit, Mia turned to Robert. "So? What did you think?"

"It was so long," he whined. "Wasn't there supposed to be an intermission? And the female lead, I've already forgot her name, I'm sure she graduated from the School of Overacting. Not to mention the fact that I didn't understand a word the British dude said." Robert was helping Mia on with her jacket. "Now you're probably thinking that I'm a cultural cretin."

"You didn't enjoy the clever dialogue and brilliant repartee?" she asked.

"What?" Robert said, and Mia started to laugh. "What's so funny?"

"I'm yanking your chain. The play sucked, Robert. Let's get out of here."

As they walked toward the car, Robert stopped in front of a

little café and asked Mia if she would like a hot drink before calling it a night. She was about to deliver her stock answer when she realized she felt no desire to fabricate an early morning meeting.

"I'm sorry you didn't enjoy the play," Mia said, as they sat down.

"Why are you sorry? You didn't write it. Or direct it. Or perform it." Robert rested his elbow on the table. His chin was in his hand. "Yes, I would say it was pretty painful, but at least it wasn't a musical."

"What? You don't like musicals?" Mia said, clutching her hands over her heart and feigning death. Robert snickered at her dramatic protest. "Tell me, which musicals have so offended you?"

"My worst experience was watching grown men and women in full makeup, bodysuits and faux fur impersonating felines, slinking down the aisles, singing songs that made no sense and trying to muddle through an incoherent plot."

"You didn't like *Cats*?" Mia shrieked.

"And what exactly is a Jellicle cat anyway?" Robert didn't wait for an answer. "I'm telling you, nobody knows. It's the eternal unanswered question."

"I think this relationship might be in jeopardy," Mia said, and noticed that Robert was utterly still, his eyes fixed on her.

"Why are you staring at me?" she asked.

"Why is it that you haven't been scooped up yet?"

"Not you too," she whimpered. Her playfulness evaporated.

"What does that mean?"

"You're trying to figure out what's wrong with me," she said. "I'm in my forties and I've never been married, so clearly there must be something wrong with me."

"Easy now," Robert said, leaning back in his chair. "I swear I'm not looking to find out what's wrong with you. I didn't mean to strike a nerve."

"But you're looking for a reason or an explanation, aren't you?"

"No. I just want to get to know you better. You must have had your share of experiences. Probably some good, some bad, like most of us. And for whatever reason they didn't work out. I'm not on a fishing expedition here, I'm genuinely interested. It would be a fair question for you to ask me."

"Sorry. You did touch a nerve," Mia said, embarrassed. "So, why have I not been scooped up, as you put it?" Mia raised her eyes to the ceiling as if she might find writing up there. "Is 'I don't know' an acceptable answer to the question?" Robert smiled, but waited still. "It just hasn't been right," Mia said, remembering her conversation with Grace.

"What are you looking for?"

"I could give you a laundry list of characteristics and personality traits that I would like in a partner, but it would probably look like everyone's list. Beyond the obvious, I'm looking for that connection that defies explanation. So it wouldn't necessarily be because he and I have common interests, or want the same things, or share the same values. It would just be because."

"Any close calls?"

"One, I suppose," Mia said and paused to reflect on it. "Not that this is some monumental revelation – it's been said so often it's cliché – but timing really is key. If I had met him ten years later, maybe things would have turned out differently."

"This necklace that you never take off," Robert said, reaching over the table and taking the crystal between his thumb and forefinger. "Did you get this from the one that got away?" Mia reached toward her neck and brushed her fingers against his. She was momentarily distracted by the surge of electricity that passed from his skin to hers.

"This? No. This is something I bought for myself," she said. "It's my security blanket. If ever I question my own strength, it reminds me."

"You get that all from a necklace?"

"It's more of a symbol than anything else."

"Do you think that having common interests, wanting the same things and sharing similar values are important?" Robert continued.

"You are full of questions tonight, aren't you?" Mia wasn't quite sure why she felt the need to shut down the conversation, but she was suddenly feeling exposed. She picked up the empty sugar packet and began twisting it between her fingers.

"Do you want to change the subject?"

She did, but in her mind she could hear Grace scolding her for making this poor guy work so hard to get to know her. Robert looked dejected.

"No, it's okay. Yes. Having similar interests and values and wanting the same things are important. If those things are missing, it could break a relationship. But they don't make a relationship." Without allowing Robert any time to respond, Mia turned the tables. "So, Robert. I'll toss the question right back at you."

"Why haven't I gotten married? I have come close once or twice but if two people want very different things and they can't reconcile their lives, then it's a no-go. I didn't want to have kids. I never did and I still don't. It's a deal breaker for a lot of women."

Mia felt the heat rise in her face as she let Robert's words sink in. She could not say that she had fallen for Robert. She had long since given up on falling. What she expected was more of a long, turbulent drop, into the patient arms of someone waiting only for her. Robert represented what might be, what could be, if she would just allow it to happen. But in the long moment before either of them spoke, Mia saw those possibilities shatter before her eyes.

"Oh," Robert said, sensing that he had upset Mia again. "You want children?"

"Why would that be so strange?"

"It wouldn't be strange. It's just that I, I don't know, I guess I just figured, you're approaching your mid-forties and—"

"Why would you assume that it's something I wouldn't want?" Silence descended again, and Mia wondered how they had gotten here. It was too soon. She didn't want to be talking about babies with this man just yet. *Let's rewind!*

"I guess I wasn't thinking. I really do like you, Mia." There was more to the thought, Mia sensed, but Robert stopped short.

"You really don't want a family?" she asked.

"Why so surprised? I have the sense that you're now thinking that something's wrong with *me*."

Mia flushed and cast her eyes downward.

"I've never felt the paternal calling," he continued. "I have two nephews and I love them to death. But I'm happy to give them back to their parents at the end of the day. I know that a lot of people don't get it. Call it selfishness, if you want."

"And you don't think you'd ever change your mind?" Mia asked, trying to reignite the hope.

"Nope. But I would never tell you to give up on your own dream."

"I've wondered if I want to have children because our society and my family say I should want them or because I really do want them. I could say that I want children because I want to live the experience of being a mother, because I feel that I have something of value that I can give to a child. And all of that would be true, but the real reason is, once again, intangible. It's an organic desire that can't be logically explained. Who knows what will be? I may have to give up on the idea someday. I'm not getting any younger, as you pointed out. But I need to accept that in my own time. I'm just not sure that I could be with someone if I knew that the possibility was already dead."

Robert took Mia's hand in his and looked at her sadly.

"Should we get going?"

No words were spoken during the short drive to her apartment. As they walked towards Mia's front door, she began to feel dread. She had said goodbye to so many men in her years of dating and never before was she filled with so much self-doubt. She rarely met a man who piqued her interest. Could she, or should she, say goodbye to Robert hoping for something that might never happen?

She fished her keys out of her purse, opened the door and turned around. She would never be able to commit to a relationship if it meant forfeiting something that had always been important to her. It was, as Robert said, a deal-breaker. Still, she reached out toward him, took his hand, and led him into her apartment. For this one time, she would allow herself to live in the moment.

CHAPTER 12

SOPHIE

Sophie dug her feet into the sand, stretched her arms and yawned. She bookmarked the page she was reading and closed the book in her lap. She had not turned a page in the two hours that she had been sitting there alone. A short distance down the beach a harried mother chased one of her kids, who made a break toward the water while the other took off in the opposite direction. The words she yelled out to both of them were caught by the wind and flung into the sky. What that woman wouldn't give to be in her place right now, she imagined. Alone on a beach with only a book and her thoughts as company. Gabe and Jessie were with friends and Alex was at the house on the phone or at the computer, where she had left him every day since they arrived in Maine two weeks earlier.

Sophie sighed. The holiday was growing tedious. She thought back to the conversation she'd had with Kate just before she left. Kate had practically begged her to stop tiptoeing around her feelings, even though they seemed trivial compared to what Kate must be going through.

◊

"For crying out loud, Sophie," Kate had said. "It's your life. It's important and I'm interested. That hasn't changed. I might be less available, but I'm listening now."

"I'm just so, I'm so—"

"Oh, for fuck's sake. Spit it out. Who knows how much time I have left."

Sophie stared at her friend in horror.

"Come on, lighten up. It was a joke."

"I'm just so bored."

"Maybe you're bored because you're boring."

"Oh, thanks. What is this, insult therapy?"

"Do you really not find any gratification in any part of your life?"

"Of course I do," Sophie said. "I love taking care of my kids. And I feel good about the volunteer work that I do."

"Uh-huh. Look, I don't doubt that you love your kids but what do you do for you? Where's the passion? Do you even know what your passion is?"

"Sure I do. Like I said. My kids, volunteering."

"And that fulfills you?"

Sophie didn't answer. The truth was, packing lunches and chauffeuring were a bore.

"There's nothing wrong with wanting more. But you have to get off your ass and act. You can't just sit back and let life happen to you. So much is out of our control, you should at least take charge of what you can."

Sophie thought about how life was happening to Kate at that very moment. "You've known me for a while, Kate. You don't know my passions?" There was a catch in her throat.

"Come to think of it, no," Kate said.

"There's something wrong with that," she said, more to herself than to Kate.

"There's nothing wrong with that. Change it, if you're not

89

satisfied. If you're bored, do something that excites you."

"I'm not even sure if I know what that is. How can I not know?" Sophie was beginning to panic.

"Relax. My guess is that as soon as you start wondering, and you let go of the guilt, the answer will come. And I bet it's going to be so obvious that you'll laugh out loud."

"What does guilt have to do with it? What do I feel guilty about?" Sophie was starting to resent Kate's self-assuredness and her presuming to know everything that Sophie felt.

"You feel guilty that being a wife, a mother and a philanthropist isn't enough."

Sophie was about to protest but instead she considered the idea. "Shouldn't it be enough? I have so much."

"There's no such thing as should or shouldn't. You don't love your children any less just because you want to pursue something that has nothing to do with Sophie the wife or Sophie the mother. Promise me that you'll at least think about what I said. It'll give you something to do when you're on the beach."

Sophie hadn't waited until she was on the beach to think about the conversation. She'd been unable to think about much else since. Standing from her chair, she put her book into her bag and walked toward the ocean. It was impossible not to feel small and insignificant when facing its enormity. Water lapped at her toes and she gasped.

"Water's cold?"

Sophie jumped and turned around.

"I didn't mean to startle you," the woman said.

"Oh, that's okay," Sophie said. "I didn't hear you coming."

The woman had large canvas bags hanging off each shoulder and was struggling to set up a beach umbrella. She was wearing a floppy wide-brimmed straw hat, sunglasses and a muumuu so enormous that Sophie could barely see the person beneath.

"Can I help you with that?" Sophie asked, not waiting for an answer as she took the umbrella from the woman.

"Thanks, dear. I can never manage these fandangled things," she said, picking up and unfolding the chair that she had dropped. Sophie drove the pointed end of the umbrella into the sand until she was sure that it was sturdy and then opened the multi-coloured shade. The woman spread out an equally colourful blanket, placed the chair on top of it and sat down with a laboured grunt. She opened one of the bags, fumbled around in it and pulled out a bottle of water.

"Thirsty?" she asked, extending her arm. "Please. Go ahead," she said when Sophie hesitated. "I have another bottle somewhere in here." She thrust her free hand into the bag again.

"Okay, sure. Thanks," Sophie said, taking the bottle from the woman's hand. She wasn't particularly thirsty but she welcomed the conversation.

"Sit," the woman instructed. "Please. I'm Jane." Sophie kneeled down on the blanket and unscrewed the top of the water bottle.

Sophie introduced herself, then brought the bottle to her lips.

"I haven't seen you here before. Do you live nearby?" Jane asked.

"No. I'm vacationing with my family for a few weeks."

"Oh," Jane said, glancing around to see where her family was.

"It's just me here today," Sophie said.

"Lucky you, got yourself a few moments of peace did'ja?" Jane laughed.

"Yes, well, the kids are with friends and my husband is back at the house working."

Sophie saw a sketch pad peeking out from one of Jane's bags. "Are you an artist?" Sophie asked, gesturing with her chin toward the bag.

"I dabble."

Jane reached for the pad and flipped it open to show Sophie an intricate drawing of an older man.

"Wow, that's incredible. I think you do more than dabble." She took the pad from Jane's hand for a closer look. "Very impressive," she said, handing it back. "Who's the man?"

"That's Henry," Jane said, looking at her drawing with what seemed like a mix of love and irritation. "He's a royal pain in the butt, but he's mine."

Sophie laughed at Jane's candour. "Do you paint as well as sketch?"

"I actually have a few paintings displayed at the gallery in town. You should come by."

"I envy your talent. I wish I had a creative outlet." Sophie looked out toward the water and sighed.

"That's a sigh of regret if ever I heard one," Jane said.

Sophie blushed. Talking to Jane was easy and comfortable.

"At one point in my life I actually saw my future in art. I did my undergraduate degree in fine art despite my father's protests. To keep him happy I took a bunch of electives in things like political science and economics. 'It's good to have them,' he would say, 'just in case.' I never knew what that meant. I had dreams of becoming a curator or something. The thought of being surrounded by art all day was so exciting."

"And then?"

"It didn't seem like there would be a whole lot of opportunity in that field. I suppose if I had been living in New York I might have had more options. But no, Dad was dying for me to go to law school." Sophie took a swig from the water bottle and stretched out her legs on the blanket. "And he could be pretty convincing when he wants to be."

"And how was law school?" Jane prompted.

"I hated every minute of it. I did well but it just wasn't me. I got married while I was still in school and when I graduated, Alex, my husband, had a good job and I just, I just never got around to getting a job. In law, anyway. I got pregnant soon after graduation, so family was the job that I took on."

"I know I just met you, Sophie, so forgive my presumption, but it sounds like your father quashed your dreams." Sophie felt a wave of indignation begin to rise, just as it did when she was with Kate.

"We don't need to get into all that," Sophie said, with a wave of her hand, wanting to close down the discussion. "In fact, what time is it? I should probably get going. The kids will be home soon and—"

"Now I've gone and offended you. I'm sorry, dear. Henry always tells me that I stick my nose in where it doesn't belong. You can stay if you want."

Sophie was already on her feet. "Not at all, Jane. No offense taken. But I really do have to go. It was great meeting you." She extended her hand to Jane.

"Likewise." Jane took Sophie's hand in both of hers and did not immediately release her hold, forcing Sophie to look her in the eye. Sophie gently slid her hand out from her grasp and trotted off toward her chair. And as she did, she noticed the noise in her head invading the end-of-day quiet on the beach.

Sophie barely heard the racket at the dinner table. Gabe was describing their neighbour's pool with the sort of enthusiasm that only an eight-year-old could express and his exaggerated gestures were making Alex laugh.

"It was so cool, Dad," Gabe said, pausing briefly to take a bite of his burger. "And after lunch we played video games on their huge TV. It was awesome."

"Don't talk with your mouth full. It's gross," Jessie said. Gabe stuck out his tongue.

"Dad!"

"Stop it, you guys," Alex said.

Sophie feigned interest in her son's detailed account of his day and offered the occasional smile or nod of the head, but she could not concentrate. She was thinking about Jane. Not only was she surprised at the unsolicited advice, she also regretted divulging all that she had within seconds of their meeting. Jane's words had depressed her. Had she thrown away everything that was important to her because she didn't have the drive to go after it? And worse, was it too late to change that truth?

"Sophie? You there?" Alex and the kids were staring at her. "I asked if you enjoyed your day."

"Oh. Sure," she said, piling the plates as she stood. She took them to the sink and began rinsing them. "I spent most of it at the beach reading. I kicked back and basically did absolutely nothing. It was exactly what I needed," she lied. "Maybe tomorrow we can do something all together."

"Mom, can we *please* go back to the Richmonds?" Gabe and Jessie sung in unison. "They're going to some cool water park," Gabe added. Sophie waited for an invitation to join them. It never came.

Alex chimed in. "I actually still have work to do, Soph, but I'm sure I'll be done in the next couple of days and then we'll do something as a family. I promise." He got up and headed for the den. Sophie turned around from the sink to find that she was alone in the kitchen.

"I need to do something," she said later that night as she and Alex were reading in bed.

"Uh-huh," he said, turning a page.

"I'm just not sure what."

94

"Why don't you go shopping at the outlets tomorrow? You usually enjoy that."

"I don't mean tomorrow, Alex. I need to do something more with my life. I need to find my passion," she said. Coming out of her mouth the word sounded stilted.

"Your passion? What are you talking about?"

"Basically, I take care of you and the kids and that's it."

"That's it? I'd say that's pretty important."

"It is important, but Kate says—"

"Oh, well if Kate says," he mocked. For reasons that Sophie didn't fully understand, Alex disliked Kate. Whenever Sophie referred to her, he greeted the name with scorn.

"What exactly do you have against her?"

"I don't know. You quote her all the time as if she's some sort of wisdom-spewing guru."

"She's a friend. Besides which, she's not the only one who says it. Jane also said that—"

"Who the hell is Jane?"

"Someone I met on the beach."

"So now you're taking advice from strangers on the beach?"

"I'm not taking advice from them, Alex, I'm just listening to what they have to say. I actually do have a mind of my own."

Alex grunted. "What's wrong with being a wife and mother? I can't think of two more important jobs."

"What I don't get is why you'd be resistant to my wanting to get a bit more out of my life. Is it because it wouldn't be all about you?" Sophie threw the covers off, got out of bed and stomped toward the door. As she left the room she caught a glimpse of Alex's pained face. The truth was, Sophie had started this conversation with Alex long before he had become an active participant, and even in her mind his reaction had always been belligerent. She replayed their short exchange and wondered if she had inadvertently led him where she expected him to go. But she had heard his words before, many times. She could no longer make excuses for him. There was no mistaking the message. Alex wanted what was best for Alex.

Sophie stretched out on the living room sofa and fell into a restless sleep. Hours later, she was startled by the clanking of dishes. She sat up slowly, rubbing her eyes. In the kitchen, Jessie and Gabe were preparing their own breakfast.

"Hi, Mom," Gabe said. "We're having cereal. Why were you on the sofa?"

"I couldn't sleep last night and I didn't want to wake Dad with my tossing and turning. Where is he?"

"In the den. Working."

"He couldn't even help with breakfast?" Sophie muttered under her breath.

"So after breakfast we're going to go back to the Richmonds, right?" It was more of a statement than a question.

"Are you sure it's okay with them? Maybe I should call," Sophie said, picking up the phone.

"It's *fine*, Mom. They invited us," Gabe whined, but Sophie was already confirming the details with Tanya Richmond.

"I'll walk you over in about an hour," she said, hanging up the phone.

In that hour, Sophie had breakfast with the kids, got dressed and packed a bag for them. Alex did not emerge from the den and Sophie didn't feel the need or desire to tell him that they were leaving. Gabe and Jessie shouted a quick goodbye before the screen door slammed behind them.

When the kids were safely in the hands of the Richmonds, Sophie continued down the road into town. She walked aimlessly in and out of the quaint shops and then found herself in front of the small art gallery that Jane had mentioned. The bells on the door clanged as she entered. A man sitting at an antique desk looked up and came over to greet her.

"Hello," he said. "Can I help you?"

"I'm not looking for anything special. I'll just browse. Is Jane, um—" Sophie hesitated, realizing she didn't know Jane's full name.

"Jane Hughes?"

"Maybe. I'm embarrassed to say I don't know her last name. I met her on the beach yesterday."

"Jane Hughes is the only Jane around here right now, so that's probably her," he said as Sophie scanned the art. Henry's face was immediately recognizable in a watercolour on the wall to her left. "Feel free to look around. Take your time."

Sophie stared at the painting of Jane's husband. He stared right back at her with tired eyes that drooped. Sophie took a step forward toward the painting, fascinated by the detail of his wrinkled face. A wry smile suggested a sort of mischievousness that Jane had alluded to. Sophie imagined Jane standing at the canvas, paintbrush in mid-air, chastising her uncooperative model who would not sit still. He's a pain in the butt, she had said, and yet it was clear to Sophie from this rendering, that the artist loved her subject. She thought about how she might depict Alex and knew that she wouldn't be able to convey the same warmth.

In the paintings on display, Sophie could see that Jane drew much inspiration from her time at the beach. There were several portrayals of seascapes and sand dunes. They were pretty, but didn't call to her very deeply. Looking at Jane's art reminded her of how scandalized she had been when an art history teacher had told the class that he didn't like Impressionist art because it consisted only of pretty pictures. He would have been dismayed to see her apartment walls at the time which displayed, in true student style, laminated posters of Degas' dancers and Monet's water lilies.

"See anything you like?" The man who had greeted her and who she presumed was the gallery owner strolled over to her.

"They're lovely," she said.

"Would you like to learn more about the artist? About Jane Hughes?" he asked, and gestured to the wall.

"Yes, of course," Sophie said. Beside the paintings was a framed panel containing a short text and a headshot of Jane. She stepped closer. Jane Hughes was a retired teacher. She had taught English for thirty-five years at a public school in Boston and picked up a paintbrush for the very first time when she and her husband moved to Maine in 1999. Just three years later, she had her first vernissage. Since that time, she had sold over four hundred pieces.

Sophie looked up at the gallery owner, who was still at her side. "So, she started her art career later in life."

"Yes, that's one of the things that makes Jane so special. It was a buried talent, and I am personally grateful that she discovered it. Are you a collector?"

"We have a few pieces but I wouldn't say we're collectors. I do love it, though," Sophie said. "For a time, I thought my career would be in the art world, but I seem to have gotten sidetracked." She was divulging personal details to strangers again. She felt a twinge of sadness. Had Kate been around to lecture her, her friend would have told her she was feeling regret.

"It's never too late," the gallery owner said.

"I wouldn't even know where to start. I took my share of art classes in university but that was a lifetime ago."

"You could start by taking more classes. You could also start visiting galleries in your city. Maybe you could even volunteer at a gallery or museum. Where are you from?"

"Montreal. We do have some wonderful galleries and museums. I don't know why I don't take advantage of them. I really should," Sophie said.

"Montreal. Been there many times. In fact, a friend of mine owns a gallery there," he said as he walked back to his desk. He took out a book from the desk drawer and flipped through it until he found what he was looking for. "Here it is," he said. "Let me write down his name and phone number for you." He pulled out a business card from his jacket pocket and flipped it over. Sophie waited as he jotted down the information and handed it to her. "Tell him that Ethan Frisch referred you."

Sophie hesitated, then reached for the card and slipped it into her purse. The flutter in her stomach was hardly noticeable. It had been so long since she had felt anything remotely like it that it was only later that day when she realized what it was: excitement.

KATE

O nce again, Kate had been stopped in her tracks by her chemo treatment. With each dose, she spent a day or two longer in bed unable to will herself to move. Sleep was the only remedy that could free her from the ravages of her body. When she felt this sick she could not imagine feeling well ever again.

Through the slits in her eyes Kate could make out the blurry figure standing at her door. She watched it approach and tried to form some semblance of a smile as Zoë came into focus.

"Mom?" Zoë was bending over her. "I brought you some toast and tea in case you were hungry," she said, placing a tray on the bedside table.

"Mmm." Kate felt the mattress depress as Zoë sat down on the bed. She could sense Zoë's discomfort. "It's okay, baby," Kate muttered, allowing her eyelids to drop shut again.

Kate's treatments always disrupted the delicate balance of the household. This last time, her usually composed, quiet daughter had flown into a rage, awakening both her and Daniel to the impact that Kate's illness was having on their family. Her daughter's words had stung, not so much because they were directed at her in anger, but because Zoë had been suffering in silence.

◆

"Doesn't anything or anyone else matter around here?" she had shouted as the five of them were finishing up dinner five days earlier. Zoë had been particularly quiet that day, but Kate had dismissed it as normal teenage moodiness. The outburst had followed a casual comment from Kate about her next treatment. Kate and Daniel looked at each other, then at their daughter. Seth and Michael hurriedly cleared the table and fled to their rooms. "It's like no one else has a life! Everything revolves around your cancer, your treatments. We can't have friends over before because you don't want their germs and no one can come near this place afterward because you're so sick. And we all have to take care of you even though you say that we don't. I'm your daughter. You're supposed to take care of me, not the other way around. And then a few weeks later we start the whole process all over again."

Kate had to pause a moment, not quite knowing where to begin.

"Listen Zoë," Daniel barked, but Kate put her hand on his arm. They waited, allowing Zoë to finish.

"Today was one of the best days of my life. I was appointed editor of the school paper. You knew how important that was to me and that today was the day I'd find out. But neither one of you asked."

Kate and Daniel both groaned. They had in fact forgotten.

"I'm so sorry," Kate began.

"I know, I know. It's the chemo. It's playing havoc with your memory. I've heard it before. And you know what else? We're all consumed with Mom being sick but no one talks about it. Not really, anyway. You just blow it off like it's some sort of inconvenience that we just have to ride out. Mom could die, you know. Hasn't anyone thought of that? You're always telling us you'll be fine. You don't know that for sure."

Daniel cringed. "Zoë! Mom *will* be fine."

Kate froze. Zoë shot her a look with narrowed and tear-filled eyes, and darted off to her room.

◆

They had not spoken about it since that night. Kate received her treatment and endured the aftermath. Only now, as she opened her eyes to see Zoë still sitting beside her on her bed, did she feel a bit more like herself. The nausea and pounding headache had begun to subside.

"I must've fallen asleep again," she said, her voice weak. "How long have you been there?" She sat up slowly and as she did, Zoë propped up her pillows.

"Not that long."

"Is this tea still hot?" she asked, picking up the cup beside her. Zoë helped her to steady the cup. The liquid, now cool, slid down her throat. It tasted like metal.

"I'm really sorry that I forgot about the editor position," Kate finally said. "I'm so proud of you. You're going to be fabulous."

"Thanks, Mom," Zoë said. Her cheeks had flushed pink. "Mom, what I said the other night, I didn't mean it. I don't mind taking care of you. I really don't. I want to help. It's just that—" Zoë hesitated.

"It's just that what?" Kate asked.

"It's just that I really miss you. I miss my mother. I know that sounds selfish," Zoë said.

"It's not selfish. You shouldn't have to be without your mother and I know I'm not always here in the way that you need me to be. None of this is fair." Kate wondered if she should venture further. She felt so tired and drained from the preceding days but thought she should seize the moment. "You're worried about me dying?"

"I don't know. Maybe. Yes. I guess I am. I mean, it's *cancer.*" Zoë was looking straight at her. "Don't you worry about it? No one ever talks about it."

Kate leaned back on the pillow and stared up at the ceiling as if searching for words. "I think I convinced myself that I would get through this a lot easier if I didn't indulge the fear. Or that if I started crying I would never stop. So I blocked it out the best I could and just forged ahead with what I had to do. And maybe I thought that I could protect you and the boys and Dad. You never really know how you're going to be in a situation like this until it happens." Kate reached out to touch her daughter's face. "But sure, I worry about it. I'm just so sorry that you've been alone with it all."

"Are you scared?" Zoë asked.

"Shitless. Mostly of not being here for my kids, not seeing them grow up, not being here for the milestones, like graduation and weddings and grandkids." Kate looked at her daughter and wondered if she had gone too far.

"You really think about that?" Zoë asked.

"I'm sorry. Too much, right?"

"Actually, not really," she said. "It scares me to know that you're scared, but it's more, I don't know, real. Everyone around here has been so weird. Somehow that's been scarier."

"What else scares you? What do you think about?" Kate asked.

"I'm scared about the same thing you just said. That you'll, you know... die."

"What else?"

"God, Mom. Isn't that enough? What else is there?" Zoë asked, but it was clear she hadn't finished. "It's like, one day we're this basically happy family, even though my brothers are so annoying, and then the next day everything is upside down. Why did it have to happen to you of all people?" Zoë lay down beside her mother and nestled into her arms.

"You know, I never ask myself that question. A lot of people do, but I think why anyone? Why *not* me?" Kate asked, her voice low with emotion. She wrapped her arms around her daughter as tightly as her strength would allow.

"I guess. Maybe what I'd like to know more than why you, is why did it happen at all? If someone smokes and gets lung cancer I can somehow get my head around that. But why did you get cancer?"

Kate had no answer. She had asked the same question. Even though she'd avoided the 'why me' phase, she still thought that there was something so arbitrary about her getting sick. At the age of fifty-three, with no family history and no other known risk factors, she was facing breast cancer. Meanwhile, her eighty-five-year-old, chain-smoking, bacon-loving father-in-law, who had never entered a gym in his life, was still kicking around like an unruly teenager.

"I don't know," she said.

"Maybe I'll get it," Zoë said in a whisper, as if not wanting to be heard. "Isn't it true that I have more of a chance because you have it?"

"We'll do everything we can to protect you," she said, hoping her voice wouldn't break. The answer was vague but Kate took Zoë's silence to mean that she was satisfied with it. She stroked Zoë's hair with one hand and wound her other arm around her waist, and the two of them drifted off to sleep.

CHAPTER 14

SARAH

Sarah was trying desperately to think of something to say. She silently implored Maggie to begin talking. The clock ticked, cars honked and braked in the street, and the office air conditioner whirred. There was so much to say, really, but the past two months had exhausted her and she could not bear the thought of delving yet again into the emotional turmoil that had become her life. She wished only that she could curl up on the couch and fall into a peaceful, dreamless sleep. Her shoulders sagged and her eyes drooped.

"Why are you so quiet today?" Maggie asked.

Sarah shrugged. "How about you start us off today," she said.

"That's kind of hard to do when I have no sense of where you're at," Maggie said, smiling.

"I'll tell you where I'm at," she said, her tone serious. "I'm exhausted. It's hard enough that I have to live inside my head all day long. Then I come here and I'm supposed to rehash everything."

When Sarah didn't continue, Maggie said, "You should know that there's really nothing you're supposed to do here. This is your space to do with what you want."

"I know that but right now there's nothing else to use it for. My mind runs on one track only. That's what's so draining."

"Why fight it? Why spend energy resisting?"

"It is hard to imagine something else occupying this mind of mine." Sarah paused. "But I would love to have a trivial, pointless conversation about nothing. A political debate with Matthew, or a light-hearted dispute over some movie I love and he hates. It would be such a relief."

"It'll happen, Sarah. This is a process. Allow yourself the time and space you need. Without judgment. And you'll get there."

"I was just telling my sister that that's exactly what I need. Just to be. I only hope that Matthew can give me the time and space," Sarah said, realizing in that instant that this was the thing she needed to talk about today.

Sarah had thought a lot about that day in the park with Emma. It had been so liberating for her that someone actually under-stood. "Tell him," had been Emma's parting words. "Tell him what you told me." But Sarah hadn't done this.

"Why do I need to tell him?" she asked Maggie after relat-ing her talk with Emma. "He should know. He is in exactly the same position I'm in."

"What position is that?"

"He lost a child. He lived through the miscarriages, just like I did."

Sarah could tell that Maggie was processing what she was hearing and preparing to say something. In the few weeks that she had been seeing her, Sarah had come to know some of her habits. Maggie would take a breath, as if about to speak, release it, rest her chin in her hand and look slightly down at the floor. Sarah would wait.

"You said that you hoped Matthew would allow you time and space. What do you mean?"

Sarah rubbed her right temple and blinked her eyes. Maggie looked at her, expressionless.

"Like I was telling my sister, Matthew wants to have an

action plan. He wants to strategize what to do next. But I'm ten paces behind him."

"You want to live it and feel it, while Matthew wants to move forward."

Sarah nodded.

"Why wouldn't you share that with him? Why wouldn't you talk to him in the same way that you talked to your sister?"

Sarah liked Maggie. She had been helpful. But she was yet another person to pummel her with questions, and today Sarah's frustration and impatience surged. "Why should I have to explain any of this to him?"

"You said yourself that the two of you are not in the same place."

"I know, but he should just know how I'm feeling."

"You expect him to read your mind?"

"Hardly. But—"

"Emma didn't know what you were going through until you told her. So why have a different expectation of Matthew?"

"Because he's in the same sinking ship as I am."

"But his experience might be different from yours."

Sarah didn't respond.

"Are you angry with him because he isn't in the same place that you are? Do you feel that he is somehow betraying the memory of your son by wanting to look toward the future?"

"No, of course I'm not angry with him. How could I be angry with... He's... How could I possibly...?" Sarah's mind was spinning. "He's been through so much too. How could I be...?"

Maggie allowed Sarah to process the suggestion.

"A couple of days ago he actually asked me if I was angry with him and I told him he was crazy."

"What was the context?"

"We were both sitting up in bed reading. He closed his book, moved over to my side of the bed and started kissing my neck in a way that could mean only one thing. It was so irritating. I told him to stop. He told me not to worry, that the doctor said it was okay, but I just couldn't take it." As she related the incident, she felt a rush of guilt. "He doesn't deserve that, I know. But for him it's business as usual. In his mind, since we can, we should."

"What do you think was holding you back?"

"I know I'm afraid of getting pregnant at this point, but obviously we can make sure that doesn't happen. So that's not really it. I guess I don't really know what it is. I just feel so sad so much of the time. Sex is the last thing on my mind. How can it be the first on his?"

"Are you angry because amidst all the pain and sadness he wants to have sex?"

"I guess so."

"And maybe, in your mind, that means that he doesn't share your feelings of loss and sadness?"

"I don't know. Maybe." Maggie's words rung truer than she wanted to admit.

Again, they fell into silence. Sarah tried and failed to organize the chaotic thoughts spiralling through her head.

"Everyone deals with grief differently, Sarah. Maybe Matthew needs to feel connected to you, the one person in the world who truly knows and understands what he's going through. And if he feels like the two of you are not really connecting emotionally it wouldn't surprise me that he would try and find you physically." Again, Maggie left some space for Sarah to absorb what she was saying before she continued.

"What are you thinking? Any reaction to what I just said?"

"I don't know what to do with any of this," Sarah finally said.

"You don't have to do anything with it."

"I just wish he felt like I do. The other night he asked me if I would mind if he went out with friends. I never used to mind that sort of thing but how could he go out and enjoy himself after all that's happened?"

"Maybe he does have some of the same feelings as you do but he's managing them differently." Maggie shifted in her chair. "Sarah, I'm wondering if you're holding back from enjoying, well, anything really, because somehow you believe it would be wrong. Feeling happy doesn't mean you're not grieving your loss. Happy and sad aren't mutually exclusive." Maggie paused. "Do you feel anything when Matthew touches or kisses you?"

"What are you getting at?" Sarah was beginning to regret the exchange.

"Are you afraid that you might actually enjoy physical intimacy with him?"

Sarah rested her head in her hand, trying to muster the energy to answer. She glanced at the clock on the table by her chair and was grateful to see that they were just about done.

"You're closing down," Maggie said.

"I'm tired. Can we come back to this some other time?"

"Sure. Why don't we do that," Maggie said as Sarah stood to leave.

As Sarah drove home, Maggie's words played over and over again in her head. What part of her, she wondered, really wasn't ready to move forward and what part was simply afraid? For the past two months she had dug her heels in, unable - but also unwilling - to climb out of the darkness, grief and devastation. Besides wanting to respect Ben's memory, she also feared the future. The unknown lay ahead and Sarah wasn't sure she could stand more disappointment. And even if she managed to look forward, she couldn't take a step, or climb out of the hole into which she'd fallen. But Matthew had tossed down a long rope, and was waiting up top for her. Perhaps it was time to grab hold. It might be the only way out.

CHAPTER 15

MIA

One week had passed since Mia had told Robert she couldn't see him anymore and in that one week she had spent every waking hour revisiting the decision. Within moments of opening her eyes on Sunday morning, the thoughts were teeming. *I failed. Again.* She had jumped the gun with Robert. She could have made it work. She was engulfed by fear, a feeling that was becoming all too familiar. *This is something I will never achieve.* She turned over onto her side and placed her hand on the back of her neck, now damp with perspiration. But wait. Having children was part of the plan so a future with Robert had to be doomed. But what if? What if she never met the right person? And forget never. Never was a lifetime away. She needed to meet that person now. She pictured herself in five years. No child and no man. She bolted upright in bed, heart racing, and gasped for air. The plan. Could she give up on the plan?

And then, again, that nagging thought that had been fleeting at first but was now trying to implant itself in her brain. She tried to let it in, then pushed it away. It was too scary. She would think about it later, when it was safe, with Grace.

Mia forced herself out of bed, moving slowly. She had to meet Grace in an hour, and she hoped that Grace would tell her what she needed to hear, whatever that was. And she needed to hear it now before she drowned in doubt.

❖

"Sleep much?" Grace asked as Mia approached the table where Grace was sitting.

"Does it show?" Mia sat down opposite her friend.

"I didn't know that you liked him that much," Grace said, guessing the source of Mia's insomnia.

"I don't," Mia said. "Well, I did, actually, or at least I thought I might, but that's not the point. There's always something blocking it. Either the feelings aren't mutual, or the timing is off, or he doesn't want to have kids, which is a new one for me. I never thought it would be so difficult to align my desires with those of a man. Everyone else seems to do it. Why the hell can't I?"

"For one thing, it's a challenge for everyone," Grace said. "I'm amazed that it ever works, frankly."

"That's pretty cynical."

"Not cynical, realistic. That's how I see it anyway."

"So should I give up?"

"Of course not. I'm just saying that I get why it's hard." Grace and Mia looked up at the waitress who had come to take their order. Without looking at the menu they each ordered their usual Sunday morning fare and then returned to their talk.

"Maybe I just made a huge mistake," Mia continued.

"Having kids is important to you. What other choice could you have made?"

"Kids are important to me. They have been anyway. But meanwhile, I may have said goodbye to someone pretty special."

"If only we lived in hindsight," Grace said. "You also might wake up one morning next to a man who makes you happy and who wants the same things that you do. Unfortunately, that's not a crystal ball hanging around your neck."

"Wouldn't that be nice. Crystal clarity." She took a breath as if she was going to say something then caught herself.

"What?" Grace asked.

"Nothing."

"Come on, don't make me beg."

"It's just something I've been tossing around in my head. I'm afraid to say it out loud."

Grace raised an eyebrow. "Just say it."

Mia leaned into the table as if divulging a classified secret. "What would you say if I admitted wanting to adopt a child on my own?"

"I'd say that's an incredible idea."

"I'm not considering it seriously," Mia said, trying to diffuse Grace's excitement. "But in the past few days I can't seem to get the thought out of my mind. There are just so many reasons not to."

"Such as?"

"Are you kidding? How would I manage as a single mom? I'd have no free time. Besides, kids are expensive. And this one would have no father. Maybe that's not fair." Mia stared at Grace waiting for a reaction. "Well? What do you think?"

"I think that would be one lucky kid."

Mia wanted to embrace her friend for the love and confidence that she consistently showed.

"Sure, it would be hard. It's hard with two parents, let alone one. But it's doable. I think you have to decide if this is a dream that you can let go of, or one you have to pursue no matter what. And in the meantime, why don't you poke around and get some information? Talk to single mothers. Visit an adoption agency."

"I thought we were just talking! I'm not there yet," Mia said, leaning back in her chair to allow the waitress to set down the plates.

"You don't have to be anywhere. You're just collecting information. I'll help you. I'll go with you." Mia scooped up some of her scrambled eggs on a piece of toast and took a bite.

"What about artificial insemination? You know, having your own child?" Grace asked.

Mia winced at Grace's use of such clinical language in the context of her having a baby. "I've thought of it. But I have to be able to visualize something before I make it happen and right now that idea is just one giant blur."

"How come?"

"A million reasons. I don't think I could go through such a long and arduous process with no guarantee that it will work. And if it did work, being pregnant alone seems like such a lonely proposition. Giving birth alone—" Mia anticipated Grace's objection and quickly added, "I know that I wouldn't be all alone. I have my family. I have you. I have friends. But still. It's not the same as having someone who's right there with you. And it's not like you'd be there in the middle of the night to go to a crying baby. And the absent father thing. If I have a kid on my own then I would be creating a new person who will have no father. I know that families come in all different shapes and sizes. I don't have a problem with anyone else doing it, but for me it seems complicated. And then the kid has to face all sorts of questions about where his or her father is."

"I'm a journalist, Mia. I could tell you all kinds of stories where the father might as well be non-existent for the amount of time he spends with his family. Or, his presence is so toxic that the family would be better off without him. You must have seen those kinds of families in your years as a reporter."

"Sure. But at least the kid could say the dad was a deadbeat or the dad was never home or the dad left home."

Grace laughed. "That would be better?"

"Well, sort of. No. I don't know. It's true that some families would probably be better off without the father. There are families who would be better off without the mother, for that matter. But it's a leap I'm not sure I could take." Mia was toying with the remnants of her eggs with her fork. "I can't even believe that we're talking about this. If you'd told me twenty years ago that I would be considering single parenthood, I'd have said you were nuts. So much for the master plan."

"There is no plan."

"Look at you. You did everything right on schedule."

"Says who?"

"Don't be dismissive. You don't know what it's like to be perceived as someone who missed the boat, who somehow got it wrong."

Grace softened. "I don't mean to be dismissive. I just wouldn't want you to miss out on something amazing because it wasn't part of some imaginary plan."

Mia sighed. "I know, I care too much about what other people think." She leaned forward, lowering her voice and pretending to gossip, "Remember that girl, Mia? She never got married. Got so desperate, she had to have a child all by herself."

"Or, remember that girl, Mia?" Grace said. "She didn't let anyone or anything stop her from getting what she wanted. What courage."

Grace always seemed to have an answer. Mia was irritated and grateful all at the same time.

"Did you talk to your parents about it?"

"No, not yet. They would be supportive, for sure. It obviously wouldn't be their first choice, but they want me to be happy."

In truth, unless she could follow the plan, one she had created so many years ago, Mia had no idea what would truly make her happy. For now, the image of a traditional family was out of reach, and she resented it. She hated that she could not achieve what seemed so simple, despite what Grace had said, and had to resort to a plan B. The thought that this child would be a compromise made Mia ache with sorrow for it.

CHAPTER 16
SARAH

I t had been ten years since Matthew first strutted into the hospital where Sarah worked. More often than not, she and her colleagues found that the pharma representatives were nuisances and Matthew was no exception. Sarah had been thumbing through a file at the nurses' station while Matthew tried to convince one of her colleagues that he only needed five minutes of Dr. Yeager's time. Sarah rolled her eyes at Gina who was trying politely to dismiss him. Matthew caught the look.

"Come on, ladies. Give a guy a break."

Sarah winked at Gina and walked away. She didn't give the charmer a moment's thought until a half hour later when he intruded on her break in the hospital coffee shop.

"Hello. Again."

Sarah looked up from her magazine. "Oh. Hi."

"Do you mind if I..." Matthew motioned to the empty chair. "Would you believe all the seats are taken?" he said, holding a cup in one hand and a muffin in the other. Sarah's eyes quickly surveyed the room. There weren't any free chairs.

"Go ahead," she said closing her magazine. "I was pretty much done anyway."

"Don't leave on my account," he said, flashing a wide smile.

Oh great, Sarah thought, he's going to try a sales job on me. "I actually do have to get back to work."

"You haven't even finished your coffee," he said, nodding at her cup. "God, I can't seem to get anyone to talk to me today. Must be this tie." He tugged at the knot to loosen it.

Sarah did have to get back to work and she wasn't usually susceptible to male wiles, but still, something kept her from getting up. "Have any luck upstairs?" she asked.

"I didn't get to see the doctor but I did get an appointment. So I suppose that's luck. Sometimes it's like getting into Fort Knox. We're not snake oil salesmen, you know." He bit into his muffin. "I'm Matthew, by the way." His hand stretched over the tabletop.

"Sarah," she said, taking it and noting the grip. That first meeting ended with Sarah excusing herself to return to work. Thoughts of Matthew lingered, however, which surprised her because their encounter had been so brief and she wasn't even able to articulate what it was about him that intrigued her.

She tried to sound nonchalant when she asked Gina about Dr. Yeager's appointment with the sales rep. "When is she meeting with him?"

"Why?" Gina asked.

"Just curious."

"Yeah, right," she said, moving toward the computer keyboard. "Next Thursday at 10 a.m."

When Matthew returned the following week, Sarah made sure to plant herself in his path. He seemed pleased to see her and didn't conceal his surprise when she mentioned that she would be heading down to the coffee shop at around 10:30 a.m. and that he was welcome to meet her if he was done with his appointment. In the course of that second meeting, Sarah fell for Matthew in a way that she had never experienced before.

Now years later, she yearned for those days when everything

was simple and they were unencumbered. Standing in the den door-way, Sarah could see Matthew lying on the couch, patting the top of Lucy's head with one hand and punching the channel changer of the TV remote with the other. She hesitated, but then walked into the room, stopping to give Lucy a quick rub behind the ears. Matthew bent his legs, leaving Sarah room to sit down at the end of the couch.

"What are you watching?" she asked.

"Nothing really," he said, his eyes still fixed on an image he would reject in a few seconds as he flipped through the channels. "It's all junk."

"How was your day?" It was small talk. Sarah cared about his day, but she was working up to something, not quite knowing how to get where she needed to go.

"Fine. You know, the same drill. Nothing too exciting."

"I remember when you used to love your job. The challenge was always such a thrill," she said.

"Yeah well, you know, I still like it I guess, but I wouldn't call it thrilling."

Sarah decided to plunge. "I'm ready. To talk about things."

Matthew turned off the TV and sat up straight. He seemed so eager that for an instant, she faltered.

"Okay," he said. "What things exactly?"

"What we're going to do. I know you've been wanting to do this for a while now, but I couldn't."

"I don't know what to do for you anymore."

"I know," she said, feeling her heart speed as Matthew moved closer to her on the cushions. "I don't know what you can do for me either. I don't even know what I can do for myself. What I do know is that I'm tired of this. I'm worn out."

"But you know what you want to do?" he asked. She could tell that he was forcing himself to stay calm.

"Not really. I want to at least try to talk to you about it.

Beyond that, I haven't got a clue."

"Talking is a good start. You've been so distant."

Sarah looked into his eyes and saw a sadness that had not been there before. Or maybe she hadn't noticed.

"Sarah, I held him too. Remember? Ben was my son too." Those were the words. But the tone said volumes more. Sarah felt a rush of sympathy and guilt: sympathy for the person before her who had suffered such a great loss, and guilt for being absent to him. It was the first time since Ben's death that he had said their son's name.

"I know." She rested her head on his shoulder.

"So let's lay out our options."

Sarah's sympathy evaporated. "Matthew, we're not deciding on a business strategy." She raked her fingers through her hair and blinked back the tears. "I'm sorry. I know that's not what you meant."

"I never seem to get the words right." The sadness was replaced by a look of defeat.

"It's not about words. It's about allowing yourself to feel what happened."

"What makes you think I haven't done that? Or that I don't do it every single day?" Matthew said, echoing Maggie. "I just don't express it like you do."

Sarah was nodding. It all made sense in her head, just like it had when she was talking to Maggie, but it was taking time to reach her gut. Matthew was quiet. Sarah assumed that he was waiting for her to speak.

"I'm afraid that if we try and have another baby, it will end the same way. And I really don't know if I can handle that. It might break me completely. But at the same time, how can we not try again?"

"What if it wasn't our own child? I know it's not something we ever talked about because we both just assumed we would have kids the time-honoured way."

"You mean adoption?"

He nodded. "How do you feel about that?"

"I'm not sure. Mixed feelings, I guess. In my head I know that being a parent is much more than biology. But in my heart... How do you bond instantly with a baby that's just handed to you? 'Here, love him.' What if I don't?"

"Remember my friend Sam?" Matthew asked. Sarah had fond memories of Matthew's colleague who had come to their home for dinner a handful of times before he and his wife moved to Toronto. She remembered how excited he had been when his wife got pregnant and how he had proudly trotted out the photos of his baby daughter.

"Sure."

"I never told you this, but when his daughter was born, his wife didn't form an attachment to her right away. She fed her and changed her and did everything she was supposed to do, but Sam said that she was just going through the motions. She kept saying that she was a terrible mother and that she wasn't normal. We all think that it's going to be love at first sight, but sometimes it isn't, even if the baby is your own."

Sarah thought back to her last visit with the couple, just after the baby was born. She never would have known. "So what happened?"

"With time, many months even, that bond developed. Somehow it just happened, but it wasn't overnight. Far from it."

"So you wouldn't be worried about feeling that way about an adopted child?"

"I didn't say I wouldn't be worried," Matthew said. "I just think that you don't know how you'll feel or what process you'll have to go through regardless of whether the kid is yours or not."

"Would we adopt a child from here or, let's say, from China or another foreign country?" Sarah asked. It was challenging enough, she thought, to get her head around the idea of mothering a child who was not biologically her own. But if he looked so different from her or Matthew, she could only imagine that it would be that much more difficult. The words "Plan B" would be writ large on the child's forehead. But she didn't share these thoughts with Matthew because she felt ashamed.

"I don't really know. For me, a baby is a baby, regardless of where he or she comes from," Matthew said, making Sarah feel worse.

"I wouldn't even know where to start. It's overwhelming." Sarah couldn't even articulate all of the questions swirling through her head. *How long would it take? How expensive would it be? Could we afford it? Would we have to travel? At what age could we bring the child home?*"

"It is overwhelming. We'd have to get the answers to our questions. But Sarah, we can't move forward until you are committed. No one is going to allow us to adopt a child if it's clear that you're choosing second best."

"If we could have a child on our own, we wouldn't be talking about this, would we?"

"Well, no. I've never been through this before, obviously, so maybe I don't know what I'm talking about. I would guess that a lot of people who adopt have had some sort of fertility problems. But I would also guess that at some point they accepted the fact that their family was going to be made differently from how they first expected. You'll have to get there, Sarah. Because a baby deserves all of you. And if we move forward on this, we need to do it as partners."

Sarah had no answer. Not just then.

CHAPTER 17
MIA

The room was austere, much like the woman sitting behind the desk. Mia doodled in her notebook, trying to busy herself, as she waited for the woman to look up from whatever she was writing. Only names had been exchanged and that had been several minutes ago. Or so it seemed. Mia had that feeling when you can't believe what's happening or where you are, so you close your eyes and open them again convinced that you will be someplace else. And so she did. But here she was still, sitting across from... *what was her name again? Kristen? Christy? Christine. That was it. What the hell was she doing?* She fought the urge to bolt.

Try as she might to dismiss the conversation she'd had with Grace, it had lodged in her brain, stirring up thoughts and fantasies until she had no choice but to make the call, if only to quiet the noise. Finally, Christine placed her pen down and leaned over her elbows across the desk. Mia dove right in.

"I'm here for some information," Mia said, "about adoption, the process, stuff like that." She grimaced at her lack of eloquence. *What an idiot, I am.*

"I can help with that. Would you want to adopt a child locally or would you prefer an international adoption?" Only then did it occur to Mia that she would have to make a choice.

"I'm not sure. I would just want to adopt a baby regardless of where he or she came from. Wouldn't it be possible to adopt the first baby available?" Mia asked.

"Actually, no. You have to choose. You can't go on both lists. It's either international or local." Christine spoke as if Mia was choosing between soup or salad.

"What's the difference in terms of the process?"

"For one thing, it can take much longer to adopt a child locally, that is, if you want a newborn. We are now treating cases that were filed... let's see," she said, typing on her computer keyboard, "four years ago. But the wait can be longer. Maybe up to eight years."

"What if I did say that I wanted to adopt locally? What then?"

"You're placed on a wait list. And after tackling a mountain of paperwork, you do just that. Wait."

"That's it? Don't you need to make sure that I can take care of a child?"

"Yes, we will do an assessment. We'll want to make sure that you can provide a permanent and secure environment for the child. We will also want to know that you feel comfortable with adoption and about discussing it with people around you, that you understand and accept that this baby will not be born to you and that you have an awareness as to what adoption entails. And of course, we will assess your financial situation. If you go the route of an international adoption, there is the additional cultural element. We will want to discuss how you will deal with this issue, how you might help the child deal with racism should that become a problem. You know, things like that." Christine's response was scripted, almost robotic. They might as well have been a talking about buying a car.

"And a single person can adopt a baby?"

"Anyone can go on the list. But we won't place infants with anyone over fifty." Mia still had a number of years before she got to fifty, but given the wait, she did not have a whole lot of time to figure this out.

"And if I wanted to adopt internationally?"

"You would first decide on the country. There are agencies here in Montreal for each country that conducts international adoptions. For example, if you chose Ukraine, then you would deal with the agency that facilitates adoptions with that country. Although—," Christine stopped mid-sentence and sifted through a stack of papers until she pulled out what she was looking for. "Ukraine actually isn't an option for you. It requires that adoptive parents be married. So, no single parents."

Mia frowned. "But these kids in foreign countries are in orphanages, right?"

"Yes, for the most part. Orphanages or foster homes."

"So an orphanage is preferable to a single parent who can provide a stable and loving home?"

"I know. Doesn't seem fair, does it?"

"Forget about fair, it isn't right." Mia visualized a nameless child gripping the rails of a crib, waiting for someone to claim him. She waited, trying to sweep the image from her mind, and Christine waited too, offering nothing more.

"What would the cost be for a local adoption?" she asked Christine, refocusing, and looking down at the notes she had been taking.

"The costs are minimal when compared with international adoption. Mostly legal fees."

"So, international adoption would be much more expensive but quicker."

"Most likely. And of course with international adoption you will have to make at least one trip to the country of origin. Possibly more."

"I can't help but feel that I would be buying a baby. It seems wrong."

"A lot of people feel that way but in reality you're paying administrative and legal fees," Christine said. "One reason why some opt for international adoption despite the significant cost is that once you've adopted the child, he or she is yours."

"Meaning?"

"If you adopt a baby locally, the birth parents have thirty days in which to change their minds. If they do, the baby has to be returned."

Mia's jaw dropped. "Returned?"

"It's devastating to the adoptive parents, for sure. But that's the risk that you would be taking."

"Does it happen often?"

"No. But it does happen."

◆

Mia hadn't been able to think about anything but adoption since her meeting with Christine. With elbows planted firmly on the desk and her face cupped in her hands, she stared at the flashing cursor on the screen. The soft hum of her computer grated. She had been sitting there for the past half hour trying to churn out an article for work but had not put a single word on the page. She pushed her chair back and spun around to face the mess that her home office had become. She remembered the puzzled look on Robert's face when she had given him a tour of her apartment for the first time. She had swung the door open and hopscotched her way over the piles of file folders on the floor, turning to see him hovering over the threshold.

"You sure are full of surprises," he said.

"I am?"

His eyes widened and he smirked. "I had you pegged as someone orderly, everything in its place. You're actually, well, you're messy!" he said, delighted with the discovery.

"I do have to clean this place up," Mia said, hands on her hips. "But it's easier to close the door."

As she recalled that conversation, she imagined that the arrival of a baby would mean that this room would have to be cleaned up. Or cleaned out, more likely. She tried to imagine what it might look like as a baby's room. It would have to be painted. Perhaps a gender-neutral, soft green. She would dispense with the typical white furniture in favour of a cherrywood crib and armoire, but she would definitely opt for the rocking chair in the corner, no matter how cliché it was. The mobile over the crib would play a classical music selection and colourful artwork would brighten the walls.

Even as she planned the baby's room, she couldn't picture herself as the mother. It's not that she didn't see herself as the maternal type. Though she wasn't drawn towards all babies and was never one to fuss over the children of friends or colleagues, Mia had developed a special bond with her sister's kids just hours into their young lives, from the moment they had gripped her pinkie with their tiny hands and what seemed like all of their strength. It had been a strange but potent experience, to be instantly intoxicated by another human being. And yet, right now as she contemplated the possibility of motherhood, she couldn't quite absorb it.

Mia turned her chair back around to face the computer and typed in the web address of the international adoption secretariat that Christine had given her. She pored over the list of countries and their adoption criteria. Like Ukraine, many countries deemed her to be unsuitable. Mia had expressed to Grace her own reservations about being a single mom, but it infuriated her to think that someone else could actually judge her. At least she wasn't a guy, she thought, as she perused the list further. Based on what she was looking at, single men wanting to adopt internationally could pretty much forget it.

Mia's eyes were drawn to the list of costs associated with each country. She gasped. In Vietnam, which seemed to be the least stringent in terms of criteria, an adoption would run her anywhere between twenty and forty thousand dollars. As she stared at the figures before her, the injustice of it all sank in. Circumstance would dictate that not only would she have her child in a non-traditional manner, she was also going to have to dip into her life savings to do it. Mia took a deep breath and released it slowly. As she did, she felt something cool slide down the front of her shirt. She fished out her necklace, which had come undone, and placed the crystal in her open palm.

"So where's the courage I need now?" she said aloud, looking at the pendant. "How am I supposed to know what to do?" She put her necklace back on, closed the adoption website and stared once again at the flashing cursor on the blank page.

❖

Mia had discussed, debated, analyzed and over-analyzed the life-changing prospect of adoption with Grace and her parents. She had not thought that she would need them at this next meeting with Christine, but as she waited, she realized that she would have liked the company. She twisted the chain of her necklace and looked around the room at some of the other faces, wondering what stories lay behind their inexpressive eyes. Mia remembered her trip to Europe a few years earlier and how the common thread that linked all of those people was that they were single. Today, in this waiting room, she wondered if the people waiting with her were bound by some kind of loss or disappointment. It was distressing to think that this is what might bring her to her child. But then, Mia watched a couple emerge from one of the offices and saw them exchange looks of what could only be described as joy. It was unmistakeable. Until that very second, she had not even contemplated the possibility that maybe, just maybe, this was not everybody's second choice. *It's my second choice.* And there it was again: doubt, trying to wheedle its way into her head and take root.

"Are these seats taken?"

In her mental ramblings, Mia hadn't noticed the two people standing beside her chair.

"They're free," Mia said, picking up her purse from the chair beside her and placing it on her lap. She and the woman glanced at one another, smiled and then looked away. The woman and the man sat down and she reached for his hand. Mia sensed that it was a reach provoked by fear, more than anything else. She decided that theirs was a story filled with pain. The woman crossed one leg over the other and Mia watched it jerk up and down. With his hand still intertwined in hers, the man placed it on her knee until her leg slowed and stilled completely. Her own legs remained immobile, even as her insides spasmed. The woman glanced at Mia and Mia turned away, embarrassed that she'd been caught staring.

"Nerves," the woman said.

Mia nodded, surprised by the candid admission, and unsure as to whether she wanted to engage this stranger or not. She was relieved when the woman turned back to the man beside her. When his phone started to ring the receptionist looked up and glared and the man headed outside to take the call.

"Have you been here before?" the woman asked, turning to Mia.

"I was here last week," Mia said.

"Seems like quite a process, doesn't it?"

"It does seem pretty involved, but I'm not really there yet." Mia tried to relax. As awkward as this was, she thought it might be interesting to talk to someone going through it.

"I'm not sure that I'm there yet either. I don't even know where 'there' is."

Mia looked at the woman who seemed to be struggling with

what to say next.

"This isn't how I envisioned having my children," she finally said. Mia was once again taken aback by her candour and the speed with which she revealed such personal information.

"Are you with anyone?" the woman asked, but immediately followed with, "Oh God, I'm so sorry. I have a tendency to overstep boundaries. In my work I get into some very personal issues with people and sometimes I forget who I'm talking to. I didn't mean to pry."

"That's okay. No, I'm not with anyone despite my valiant efforts," Mia said, placing dramatic emphasis on the word valiant. She and the woman laughed. "This isn't the way I had envisioned having a child either."

"You're still young," the woman said. "Maybe it can still happen the way you want it to."

"Maybe. But I'm just worried that I might wait too long. And then it'll be too late."

"Do you ever take yourself through the worst case scenario? Like, what if you were never to have kids? Do you ever think about that?"

"Sure I've thought about that," Mia said.

"And?"

"There would be tremendous sadness."

"For me too. For me, it's unthinkable."

Mia remained quiet as she thought about the prospect of missing out on being a parent. She had turned to adoption as a way to ward off that possibility. But sitting in this waiting room alone, embarking on the journey of single motherhood seemed to be bringing her equal amounts of sadness.

"So you're sure about adoption?" Mia asked.

"Sure? God no. But there's not a whole lot I'm sure about these days."

"And you're considering adoption because you—" Mia

started to ask, but noticed the woman recoil, ostensibly less comfortable talking about herself than she was probing into the lives of others. "You don't have to talk about—"

"No, it's fine," the woman said. "I can't very well shut down when I've bombarded you with all sorts of intimate questions. I've gotten pregnant a number of times, but—." She hesitated. "Well, it just never worked out."

"I'm sorry," Mia said, surprised by the empathy she was feeling toward this woman she had met only moments ago.

"I have to say, it's been hell. I promised that I would keep an open mind. That's why I'm here." She looked toward the door where the man had left to take his call. "But it's all so uncertain."

Mia could relate all too well to that sense of uncertainty. She couldn't know if she would eventually meet someone and have a child in the traditional way, in the way that she had always hoped she would. For all she knew, it would never happen. After all, it hadn't yet. And the inability to accept uncertainty over what lay ahead was what had brought her to this waiting room today. And yet, even as she waited, she began to wonder what she was doing there.

"It must be so comforting to be able to do this with someone," Mia said. "You're lucky to have a partner through all of this."

"I guess so. But you have to be in the same place at the same time and that isn't always a given. You have to reconcile your own feelings with someone else's," the woman said. "But yes, I can't imagine doing this alone," she said, then blushed with shame. "I'm sorry. I just think that you're brave. I admire you." Mia didn't quite know how to respond so she said nothing.

"I'm hoping that there will be some sign from on high to lead me in the right direction," the woman continued. "I don't know, maybe not everyone is meant to be a mother. Maybe it's just not in the cards for me."

"Meant to be? In the cards?"

The woman groaned. "I'm starting to sound just like my mother. I'm pretty sure I don't buy that crap either."

"At some point," Mia said, speaking as much to herself as to the woman beside her, "your gut kicks in and tells you what to do. At least that's what I'm hoping. But either way, I'm starting to think that fear is an inescapable part of this." Mia felt her necklace slip and caught it before it slid off. "The clasp must be broken," she said, examining it. "It keeps coming off."

"It's lovely," the woman said. "You know what they say about the energy crystals carry. Could be some sort of sign that it keeps falling off."

"I'm way too practical for that kind of stuff. I don't believe in signs or the powers of crystals any more than I believe that something is meant to be. But I will say that this crystal has been a source of strength for me," she said, holding it up to the light. "Having it around my neck reminds me that I can in fact be a woman of valour." Mia winked to undercut the earnestness. She didn't know if it was her necklace or her conversation with this stranger, but the more she shared, the more the confusion began to lift. It was subtle, but unmistakable. She closed her palm around the necklace and shook her head.

"You know, I don't think I can go through with this," she said, slowly at first and then with conviction. "I don't want to do this." The excitement in her voice seemed to bewilder her listener.

"Why not?"

"It just doesn't feel right. I feel pressured by time, but that isn't a good reason," Mia said.

"And you're happy about this discovery?"

"Yes. No. I don't know. Relieved, I guess." Mia paused to gather the thoughts that were now flying through her mind at warp speed. "With every fibre of my being I hope there is a man in my future. I hope that he and I can have a family together. And if it doesn't happen, I will be devastated. But I'm okay with that." Mia was

131

baffled by her own words, not quite sure how she was arriving at this conclusion. "It must sound kind of strange to hear that I'm okay with devastation, but this, this—" Mia gestured to her surroundings. "It's not me. Not what I want. Not now anyway. I know that in my heart, so how can I go ahead with it? There's another life involved. It wouldn't be fair."

"You're sure?"

"No, I'm not sure!" Mia said.

"Why the sudden epiphany?"

"I don't know. And I'm not sure that it's all that sudden. I think I'm finally admitting that this option was motivated by panic."

"Seems to me the only thing we are both sure about is that we're not sure about anything," the woman said.

"I've spent so much time trying to make uncertain things certain. What a relief it would be to stop trying. It's tiring."

"So you think you'll be okay with not knowing?"

"Well, not overnight. But I hope that I can get there. I have to remember to focus on what's good about the unknown."

"How is it good?" the woman asked.

"The last man I dated was a guy I met in yoga class. It was like any other Sunday. I went to class just as I did every week and I walked out with a new person in my life. I had no idea that would happen. The unknown contains possibility."

"I never thought about it that way. It's true that anything can happen. At any time. Anywhere."

"I probably won't be able to eliminate the panic completely. But I hope that maybe, just maybe, I can reach a place where I feel a sense of, a sense of—"

"Peace?"

Mia sighed. "Yes."

"It feels like forever since I've had that," the woman said. "Peace would be nice." She closed her eyes and seemed to be imagining it. "So what do you do next?" she asked, opening her eyes again.

"I guess I start by telling Christine that I don't need to meet with her today. And then I walk out of here and, I don't know, go do something completely mundane, like the laundry."

"And you feel good about that?"

"As good as I can right now," Mia said.

"I have to say, I'm almost envious. The idea that I could choose a path and feel at ease with what I've chosen. That doesn't seem likely to happen any time soon."

"It will. It might even be happening right now, and you don't even realize it. And then something will just click and you will know what you need to do."

"Hopefully sooner rather than later. I feel like I'm living in Nowhere Land, and the weather here is getting pretty damn stormy."

Mia got up to leave. She felt good. Through all the machinations and logical analyses, she'd ignored what she needed to trust the most. It was not until she'd told the woman sitting beside her that she should listen to her gut that she'd started to hear what her own gut was saying.

"Here, why don't you hang on to this for a while," she said and opened her palm toward the woman.

"Your crystal?" The woman placed a palm over her mouth. "I couldn't possibly take it."

Mia lowered the woman's hand and dropped the necklace into it. "I'll tell you what," she said. She opened her purse and began rummaging through it. "Give me a call sometime and we can reconnect." Mia pulled out a business card and handed it to the woman. "I know that we haven't been talking for very long but you were here for a turning point for me and I'd like to know when you reach yours. You can give my necklace back to me another time."

"I don't know what to say—" The woman paused to look at the card. "Mia."

"It's not a magic crystal," Mia said, grinning. "But like I said, when I was feeling weak, it reminded me of the strength that I do have. So maybe you can use it to find yours."

She turned towards the door. The woman rose too and, taking Mia's hand, pulled her toward her and embraced her.

"Thank you," the woman said, as she released her hold.

"Good luck—" Mia hesitated, realizing she didn't know the woman's name.

"I'm Sarah."

CHAPTER 18
KATE

"Baby steps," Kate said aloud as she was getting dressed. They were Angel's words and Kate often called upon them, simple as they were, when she needed reassurance. It had been ten days since the last treatment and she was beginning to feel somewhat human again. Now she would have to begin the ritual of making herself look somewhat human again. "Baby steps," she said again as she sat down at the vanity in the bathroom to apply her makeup. She stopped and stared at herself in the mirror as she replayed that conversation. Angel was pregnant when Kate had last seen her. Kate tried to recall how far along she had been, but wasn't even sure that Angel had told her. She had asked her about the birth on a couple of occasions, but Angel always shifted the conversation back to Kate.

"That's why she left," Kate said, and saw her weary eyes widen in the mirror. "Did she have her baby?"

"Ready to go?" Daniel asked, popping his head into the bathroom.

"Almost. I just have to transform myself from an emaciated and pale cancer patient into a ravishing beauty. Should take no time at all."

"Um, great. I'll wait for you downstairs."

Daniel was thrilled when Kate had suggested they take a walk, just the two of them. She wasn't sure if she had the energy to reach the end of the block, venture all the way around it or further, but she needed to get out of the house. When Kate had told Daniel what she and Zoë had talked about, their conversation did not go much beyond their daughter. He had been stoic, his reaction no more emotional than if she had related what she'd seen on the news. Kate had learned an important lesson from Zoë – that ignoring the ugliness of her illness didn't make it less grisly. So she knew that she and Daniel had to stare it down together.

Kate pulled up the collar of her jacket as she and Daniel set out down the street. She took his hand. Autumn hung in the air but their neighbour's kids were still out on their bikes. Kate heard their fading hello as they whizzed by. She stopped to wave.

"This feels good, the crisp air. Someone looking at us might even think everything is normal."

"Everything is normal, Kate," Daniel said.

"Really? Cancer is normal? I sure as hell hope not."

Daniel frowned. "Can't we just spend a bit of time together without bringing it up?"

Kate dropped Daniel's hand. "Oh, I'm sorry," she said sharply. "Is my cancer annoying you?"

"No, Kate. It would be nice to take a break and live for just a few seconds as if it wasn't the centre of our lives."

"That's funny," she said, "I kind of feel like we never talk about it. Zoë feels that way too. It's as if this is nothing more than a nuisance."

"That's ridiculous. Of course it's more than that," Daniel said. "Our world fell apart the day you were diagnosed," he snapped, taking Kate completely by surprise. They neared the end of their street. "Where to?" he said, resigned. "Are you tired? Do you want to turn back?"

Yes, she was tired. Exhausted, really. Not so much from the walk but from the months of treatment. The chemo had been difficult, but it was more the self-imposed isolation that was most painful. Her family had seen the violent effects of the drugs, but she hadn't allowed them to see the real damage of the illness: the fear and uncertainty that was with her every second of every day. She had shared some with Zoë, but she had still maintained control.

"Let's keep walking," she said. The silence between them was strained, but Kate did not want to be the first to speak.

"You never really allowed me to see that your world was falling apart," Daniel said.

"What was I supposed to say? How would it have been helpful had I told you that I wake up scared and I go to sleep scared?" This script sounded just like the one that she and Zoë had read.

"It probably would have freaked me out," Daniel replied. "But you're impervious to everything around you. It's like you're just going through the motions." Daniel paused and took a deep breath. "Please tell me what you need, Kate. I'm clueless at this point. Obviously I can't do this without your guidance. I just never know what to say or how to act. I don't know how to fix this." His voice sounded pained.

Kate took his hand in hers again. "You can start by realizing that you can't fix this. What I need is for you to listen. Really listen and you'll hear what I need."

"I do listen."

"Okay, well maybe I've been speaking a bit cryptically, I'll give you that. But when I tell you that I need you to come with me to my appointments, I don't just mean that you have to show up. I need you to be present. If you're there flipping through the pages of a magazine, you might as well not be there." Kate could see by the look on Daniel's face that he was hurt. "I need you to talk to me, distract me, tell me something funny."

"Something funny? You feel like laughing during chemo?"

"Actually, that might be nice. God, it's been a long time since I've laughed, since I've had one of those can't-catch-your-breath belly laughs."

"It does feel like a long time since I've heard your laugh. And it's so contagious. You can get me going and I don't even have to know what you're laughing about." This made them both chuckle and the tension eased.

"You always seem so in control. Nothing fazes you," Daniel said.

"Hardly," she answered, but she knew what he meant. She almost never let on how fazed she felt. Though Kate had flailed a bit as a teen and in her early twenties, she had become the level head in their relationship. She had assumed the title, almost without knowing it, and she and Daniel had gotten used to it. Which is why, she realized, Daniel was so awkward in the role. And which is why she had tried so hard not to let go of it.

"So what now? Where do we go?" He looked like a lost child.

"I guess we head home," she answered, knowing full well that it wasn't what he meant. Truth be told, Kate had no idea where to go from there.

CHAPTER 19

SARAH

Sarah couldn't stop thinking about her conversation with Mia. She realized how nervous she must have been. It had always been a struggle to probe her personal life with a friend, let alone a stranger. It had even been a challenge talking to Maggie, at least at the beginning. It's not that she was uncomfortable talking about personal stuff. She did that all the time at work. But not her stuff. Mia had not even known her name. She wouldn't judge her, wouldn't inject her own values into the mix. God bless her family, but she could no longer stomach their opinions. Her parents wanted her to feel better. She knew that. But she couldn't handle one more invitation to go shopping to "get her mind off things."

Sarah sat at her kitchen table staring at the crystal pendant. If she added up the amount of time she spent at the kitchen table brooding over a cup of coffee over the last few months, it would probably be days. Meeting Mia had ignited hope in her. She didn't know if she was any closer to her gut today, but Mia had said that it had been a slow process even though the revelation seemed to come about suddenly. Mia had left the waiting room with a buoyant step and Sarah looked forward to the day when that same sense of relief would come to her.

Sarah understood the urge to know things for certain. The

other day she had bombarded Dr. Kerr with questions, begging for definitive answers: "Will I get pregnant again? Yes or no? What are the chances that I will eventually be able to carry a baby to term? Good or not good? Could you quantify those chances? Better than fifty per cent? Better than seventy-five? Should I try again? Yes or no?"

The answers, of course, remained vague. It drove Sarah mad with frustration.

After the meeting at the adoption agency three days ago, Sarah could tell that Matthew was treading carefully, hiding his excitement. There was so much to think about that Sarah couldn't talk about it just yet. "Can I ask a favour?" she had asked Matthew as they were driving home. "Can we agree not to mention this for twenty-four hours?"

"Okay," he said, but Sarah caught the pain on his face, and again, felt guilty about being the cause. When the twenty-four hours elapsed, Sarah was sure that Matthew would pounce, but he said nothing. She knew that he was eager to begin any process that would lead to fatherhood, but for her, he'd put on kid gloves. Again, she felt that she was to blame.

Sarah spent a lot of time with Maggie trying to figure out what was blocking her from forging ahead with Matthew to build their family. Maggie understood why Sarah would want her own children. She told Sarah her feelings were entirely normal. But if they could uncover and work through the real obstacles to another pregnancy, Sarah might clarify what she might do.

"Is it important for you to be pregnant or to have a child?" Maggie had asked the day before, and Sarah initially thought the either/or question to be flippant.

"There's more to it than that," Sarah had answered.

"Of course the issue is complex, but let's look at this. If you can't carry a pregnancy to term, do you still want to have a child? And if you do, what are your options? There's adoption, there's surrogacy."

"That's a huge if. Who said that I can't carry a pregnancy to term?" Sarah herself had doubts that she could carry a pregnancy to term and she had already told Maggie that she could not risk another loss. But Maggie's encapsulation seemed to reduce her circumstance to a series of yes or no answers. These questions, now coming from someone else's mouth, brought with them new pain.

"You don't know for sure. Right now, you can't know for sure," Maggie responded, ignoring the edge in Sarah's tone.

"Surrogacy," Sarah said. "We haven't even talked about that. I don't know. I didn't even know that was legal."

"I'm certainly not an expert in that area. You would have to look into the legal issues if this is something that you wanted to explore."

Sarah didn't say anything for a while. As usual, Maggie waited.

"If you're asking whether I would adopt if I couldn't have my own child, then yes, I would adopt. Surrogacy, regardless of the legalities, somehow seems so... it seems too... would it be politically incorrect to say 'weird?'"

Maggie laughed. "This is the last place you have to worry about political correctness, Sarah. But you might want to think about why you'd be uncomfortable with it."

In what amounted to a plea to turn off her brain, Sarah had told Maggie how tired she was of thinking and feeling. Now, here at her kitchen table, she was still immersed in analysis. Her thoughts turned to what that life had been like before this crisis. It wasn't that long ago, and yet it seemed like a lifetime away. But it was not so far away that Sarah couldn't remember how much she liked her life.

Some people thought Sarah's job was depressing, but Sarah did not feel that way. There were sad moments, but also moments of great joy and triumph. She felt gratification knowing that she may have eased someone else's pain, even if only slightly, that she brought a smile to someone's face in a stressful time, that she was a comfort to those whose lives had been callously upended. Sarah had thought therapy would be a waste of time but, as it turned out, Maggie had brought her that same sense of repose. And more than ever, she realized how indispensable that would be in connecting her to her gut.

Sarah couldn't help but feel another pang of guilt, this time for having abruptly left her job and disappearing without explanation. It felt like there was no choice, but she had yanked security away from those people who relied on her. She hadn't been able to contemplate returning to work. Every morning, she woke up drained, unable to do much for anyone. She had told herself that when everything was back on track, whatever that meant, she would return to her job. But lately, she was thinking that maybe work was the very thing that would get her back on track. For the first time in a long time, she would focus on something else, on someone else. Perhaps then, things would crystallize as they had for Mia.

The key clicked in the door. Lucy responded with a yap. "Hi," Sarah yelled from the kitchen. She could hear Lucy's faint whimpers of pleasure. Matthew always knew just where to scratch behind her ears.

"Hi," Matthew said, walking into the kitchen with Lucy trailing behind. "How was your day?" He picked up the mail on the kitchen counter and sifted through it.

"Fine. Yours?"

"Fine." He dropped the stack of mail, not bothering with any of it, and opened the fridge.

"So, I was thinking," Sarah said.

Matthew looked over at her and shut the fridge door. The look of anticipation on his face made her feel bad. "Sorry, Matthew. I was just going to ask you to be patient for a little while longer while I get used to the idea of adoption."

"Okay." The word dripped with disappointment. "So what

were you thinking then?"

"That it's time to go back to work. I need to get back to my normal life and just live for a while. I miss it."

"Oh. Well of course you should. Whenever you're ready. But are you sure that you can be in that sort of environment right now?"

"I know you see me as fragile. And I was for a long time. But I think it will be good for me."

"Probably. It's just that you give so much to your patients."

"Well, that's what I do. I'm a nurse. That's what nurses do."

"I just want to make sure that you have something left for, well, the rest of your life."

"Haven't I always, Matthew?"

Matthew sat down on the chair beside her, pulled her onto his lap and wrapped his arms tightly around her.

"You have. But just remember. You're my Angel too."

CHAPTER 20
SOPHIE

Since they returned from Maine two weeks ago, Sophie could not have a conversation with Alex without it blowing up into an argument. When she announced to him that she wanted to take a course in curatorial studies to see if it was something she would like to pursue more seriously, he scoffed. When she told him that the gallery owner in Maine gave her the name of a gallery in Montreal, and suggested she might try to get some sort of job there, he sneered. He never really explained his opposition. She could do whatever she wanted, he said, so long as she didn't neglect her family.

His patronizing words enraged her. "What is this, 1950? Am I Doris Day?" He paid little attention to her fury, but the list of evening work meetings, dinners and benefits grew, and he expected her to attend.

"And by the way," he added, "I took on a new client who spends much of his time in Florida, so I'll be travelling a lot."

"I get it, Alex, you're going to make this as difficult for me as possible. What I don't get is why?"

Alex didn't answer, but in a flash, she understood that she had answered the question in Maine. It was hard for her to accept or believe that the man she had married could be so selfish, that he held so little respect for her. She wondered if Alex had changed over the

years, or if he had always been this way. Thinking back to their court-
ship she remembered how he had encouraged her to quit law school
because she hated it. At the time, she believed that it was out of love,
that he didn't want to see her unhappy.

"I have to finish what I've started. It's not like me to quit," she had said.

"Why not? You don't like what you're doing. Besides which, once I graduate, I'll get a great job and you won't have to work any-way. So what's the point?"

Sophie had laughed at his hubris. "You're pretty sure of your-self." It hadn't occurred to her that he was mapping out her future on his own. When she had suggested she might go back into the fine arts, Alex parroted her father, telling her that it was a dead end. The paradox was glaring. Fine arts was a dead end, but if Alex had his way, she would never go anywhere.

◇

Sophie was surprised to find the babysitter still sitting in front of the TV when she strolled into her house at 9:30 p.m. The joy she had felt leaving her class just twenty minutes earlier evaporated. *He's doing this on purpose. Heaven forbid he should come home to be with his children.*

Sophie walked upstairs and stood over Gabe's bed for a few moments, pulling up the covers over his shoulders. In the hallway, light was streaming out from under Jessie's door. "Jess, what are you still doing up?" she said, knocking first and then opening the door without waiting for a response. Jessie was in bed with her nose in a book. She didn't look up. "Come on, Jess. You have school tomorrow. Lights out." She closed the door again.

She walked into her room, flopped down on her bed and kicked off her shoes. Then she reached for the phone.

"Hello?" Kate's voice was faint.

"I woke you. I'm so sorry. I wasn't thinking," Sophie said.

"Don't worry about it. I can't sleep anyway. What's up?"

"Nothing much. You?" Whenever Sophie called Kate, she treaded carefully at first so that she could gauge where Kate was at. If she was having a bad day, Sophie would not burden her with her own issues. Kate usually grew frustrated with Sophie's caution but lately, Sophie could tell that the cumulative effect of the treatment was depleting her.

"Just tired, but otherwise not too bad," Kate said.

"Remember that conversation we had before I left for Maine? About finding passion? It happened."

"That's wonderful," Kate said. The words were what Sophie wanted to hear but the tone was empty.

"I really didn't have to look all that hard. It was always there, just buried." Sophie sped through an account of the past weeks knowing that Kate's attention span was limited.

"You moved fast," Kate said in response to Sophie's proud declaration that she had already enrolled in a class.

"I had to. I got in just under the wire."

"And what does Alex think about all of this?" Kate liked Alex no more than he liked her, so Sophie rarely spoke of him. When she did, she usually glossed over what Kate referred to as his boorish behaviour. Kate felt Alex was controlling and guided by self-interest and Alex felt that Kate meddled in their personal business and tended to preach about things that she knew little about. Sophie was usually defending one to the other but tonight she couldn't manufacture any defence where none existed.

"He pretty much hates it," Sophie said. "He can't stand the fact that I have interests outside of him and my kids. I sort of can't believe it. It's so, it's so—"

"Cruel?"

Sophie knew that Kate was never one to mince words but

when she delivered them with such veracity, they hurt.

"So what are you going to do?"

"What do you mean? I'm taking this class and maybe at some point I'll contact that art gallery—"

"What are you going to do about your marriage?"

"My marriage?"

"You're living with a guy who couldn't give a shit about your happiness. That doesn't bother you?"

Sophie went silent. She had called Kate to share the excitement of what she had discovered, not to attack Alex. "I guess I should let you go," she said, wanting desperately to flee.

"I am feeling tired," Kate said.

When Sophie hung up the phone she thought it ironic that on a day when she had taken such a momentous step, she felt utterly alone. The progress she had made that day was invisible from the outside. She had enrolled in a class. But for Sophie it meant much more, and it had been thrilling. She expected Alex to blast her, but she had hoped that Kate would understand. Sophie wanted to be forgiving of her friend but lately she had to frequently remind herself of why she liked this person. She and Kate initially had a professional relationship when she and Alex were buying their house but it had evolved into a friendship. Kate was bold and fiery and Sophie had watched in awe as she went after the sellers like a barracuda, wrangling over the price and terms until they ultimately succumbed. Kate was everything that Sophie wasn't and, thinking about it now, she had been drawn to her for that very reason. Kate had moxie and Sophie hoped that some of it would rub off on her. But being on the receiving end of Kate's offensive didn't feel particularly good, and as Sophie lay on her bed she felt her resolve begin to waver.

What am I doing? She knew that a relentless pursuit of what had been ignited in Maine would damage her marriage. It was already doing just that. But when she was able to maintain her self-respect, she knew that she could not bury what she had only just uncovered. Still, she knew that if she didn't have Alex's support she wouldn't be able to do it. She scolded herself for having become completely reliant on him. It was almost as if he had designed it that way, she thought, allowing herself to see the possibility of his ulterior motives. He might agree to finance a class or two, a babysitter here and there, but if she wanted to go back to school full time, she was beginning to think that he would do everything he could to prevent it from happening.

Sophie sighed. She had become one of "those women." Those women that she and her friends had always disparaged. Women who bided their time in university, hardly studying, waiting to marry the man who would pave their way down easy street where they could indulge themselves in luxurious living without lifting one diamond-ringed finger. It had not been her intention but here she was. And she didn't know how to get out.

CHAPTER 21

KATE

The celebration had come to an end. After Kate's last chemotherapy treatment, she and Daniel clinked glasses, hers with water, his with sparkling wine, and toasted her health. She had made it through hell. Daniel had accompanied her to her last treatment and talked right through it. It was as if he'd come uncorked, and since that discussion a few weeks back, he unleashed everything he thought about like a live volcano. He wanted to know everything Kate was going through, too. She would have thought his interest was feigned, given the about-face, but his tone and expression were completely sincere. At first, it overwhelmed her, but she had asked for it.

Kate originally thought the celebration might be premature. She still had twenty-five rounds of radiation to undergo, so she was far from done. But Daniel insisted, saying that the end of chemotherapy was a milestone that required recognition. Hesitant as she may have been, Kate liked the idea of celebrating. She was ready to move forward and put an end to this awful chapter.

Despite this newfound involvement, Daniel seemed a bit surprised when Kate asked him to go with her to a lecture on cancer and body image, but he acquiesced easily enough. They had been doing better together, but there was room for improvement in the way that they interacted. This wasn't all Daniel's doing, Kate acknowledged.

This lecture might help her to find a way to express the struggle that she was having with her undeniable physical mutilation.

The person reflected in the mirror, when Kate dared to look, appeared older than fifty-three. Lines had formed across her forehead and her eyes told a story of anguish and worry. Daniel used to say that her eyes had both a seductive and innocent quality. Now they were permanently red and drooped with fatigue. Kate had welcomed the first signs of hair coming back on her scalp, though it was little more than a quarter of an inch of grey fuzz. She panicked at first, wondering if she had lost the blonde cascades that Daniel and she both loved. She chided herself for lamenting something so trivial compared with what she could have lost, but she was still relieved to learn that the colour loss might be temporary.

Before cancer, Kate had been comfortable with her body, including its imperfections. And Daniel had readily displayed his appreciation of it. But now Kate undressed modestly in her room, turning her back to her husband so that he wouldn't see the incision or her frail body. In bed, Daniel often put his arms around her or caressed her back, but that had been the extent of their physical intimacy for months. Kate recoiled from any type of advance that Daniel made, and eventually he stopped. She was frustrated with him, accusing him of being oblivious to how she was feeling. But Kate withdrew from him even when she was not feeling sick. She wished she could explain to him how her body had somehow become a separate entity, a site of invasive procedures that no longer belonged to her. Feeling any pleasure in this damaged mess was unimaginable.

The lecture included a doctor, a psychologist and a cancer survivor named Erica. Her testimony was the most compelling because Kate could relate on a visceral level to everything she talked about, from hating the label "survivor" to facing devastating physical changes. Erica joked about how she was grateful she didn't have a partner who would also have to adapt to her new physical self. During her treatment, she had hated her body, teeming with toxic chemicals, so she was hard-pressed to see why someone else would want it. Erica reported feeling angry and resentful that her body had betrayed her. Sex or the idea of romance seemed beyond reach. Even now, with some distance from her illness, she worried about letting another person see the scars that her cancer had left.

Kate saw Daniel shift in his seat as Erica spoke. She could understand his discomfort, but she was glad that he was hearing the words she had been unable to articulate.

When the lecture ended, Kate asked Daniel what he thought.

"It wasn't easy to listen to. But it opened my eyes."

As the two of them stood to put on their coats, Kate scanned the room. The doctor and psychologist were talking with Erica and the three turned as another woman approached them. Erica's face brightened and soon the two women were embracing. They held each other tight, as if they had not seen one another for a long time. It was only when they let go that Kate recognized the woman's face.

"Angel." Kate whispered. "My Angel."

"What?" Daniel asked.

But Kate was already running down the steps of the amphitheatre, taking them two at a time, leaving Daniel to follow. "Angel!" Kate yelled midway down the steps. The four people, now in conversation, looked up. "It's Kate," she explained, reaching the stage. Angel had made an impact on her, but suddenly Kate wondered if she would actually remember her. To Angel, she was one of hundreds of patients.

"Of course. Hello, Kate," she said. And like Erica, Kate drew her into her arms. When Angel stepped back, she looked at Daniel and extended her hand.

"I'm Sarah Hoffman. Or Angel, as I'm known in this place," she said with a smile. "We met at Kate's first treatment."

"Yes. Nice to see you. And thank you. You've been helpful to

Kate, even in your absence." Then he turned to Kate. "Why don't I run and get the car and leave you two to catch up for a few minutes. I'll meet you out front?"

Kate agreed and immediately turned back to Angel.

"So how are you doing, Kate?"

"I'm doing really well. I'm happy to say that I finished my chemotherapy and I have to thank you because thinking of you got me through it. I kept wishing you were with me, but in some sense you were. I just have to do radiation and then I am done."

Angel cast her eyes downward and cleared her throat. "That's wonderful, Kate," she said, trying to smile. "You look good."

"I still have a ways to go," she said, running her hand over her hair. "I loved Erica's story of the struggle to reclaim her body. I'm in the throes of that now. And how are you? You're back at work, I guess. You left so suddenly I wasn't quite sure what had happened but you must have had your baby. How is that going?"

Angel winced. "I lost it," she said.

"Oh my God. I am so sorry. That must have been—."

"Yes, but we're doing much better now," she said, smiling stiffly. "I'm happy to see you, Kate."

Kate didn't know what to say to this person who had come to mean so much but who was also unknown to her. She longed to sit down and ask about her life, but Angel wasn't her friend and didn't need her for that.

"I hope that everything works out," Kate said, putting her arms around Angel once again. "You give so much to others, it is only fair that you get your due."

Angel nodded. "I'll see you soon, Kate," she said, before turning to join her colleagues.

◇

The silence on the way home, interrupted briefly by Daniel's swearing at an inept driver, was deafening.

"I'm afraid that you won't be attracted to me anymore," she said suddenly.

The silence grew.

"I am attracted to you," Daniel said after a few more fraught seconds. "I seem to remember trying and trying to show you that."

"You did," Kate said, recognizing for a moment how her rejections must have felt. "But you haven't seen me. You've seen the bald head and you've seen me heaving over a toilet, but this body, it's a train wreck. Even I don't recognize it. What if it's, you know, different between us?"

"I'm nervous," Daniel admitted. "But you have to give me a chance. Give us a chance, really."

It was what she wanted to do, what she had to do. Kate's eyes welled with tears.

CHAPTER 22

SARAH

Had Sarah been the lead in one of those maudlin movies she abhorred, an angelic child at the table next to her would remind her of why she so desperately wanted one. He would be sipping a hot chocolate, asking his mother with some trepidation if he might also have a cookie. She would smile lovingly and tousle his hair, as she dug into her purse for money. He would give her a peck on the cheek before running off to buy his treat. While she waited for him to return, she would bask in the joy of motherhood.

Instead, Sarah witnessed a noisy brat ignoring his mother's attempts to quiet him and whose wild gesticulations tipped his cup of hot chocolate onto his mother's lap. She jumped to her feet, shrieking his name and grabbing a bunch of napkins to sop up the mess that was now dripping down her jeans. Oblivious, he pulled out a toy car from the pocket of his sweatshirt and sent it careening through the puddles of hot chocolate on the table.

"Jason! Stop it!"

"I want a cookie," he whined, without skipping a beat. "And another hot chocolate. I barely got to taste it."

"We're going home." She swung her purse over her shoulder and seized the hand of her son, who was now pulling hard in the other direction. She gave his arm a yank.

"You're hurting me!" he cried. But finally he settled down, and followed his mother out of the café.

Sarah blew on her coffee. She welcomed the quiet, broken only by the low buzz of chatter and the soft music, which she was now able to hear. The portrait of maternity had not been sweet, but still, she felt that familiar tug of desire.

She put down her cup and glanced at the door. The person she was waiting for stepped in and scanned the coffee shop. Sarah waved and stood up.

"Hi," Mia said. She approached the table and gave Sarah a warm hug. "Let me grab something and I'll be right back."

Sarah sat down again and slipped her hand into the pocket of her jacket. She felt the smooth surface of the crystal, which she carried with her wherever she went. She had kept her conversation with Mia and the crystal to herself, knowing that the power of both would somehow be diluted if she told anyone. Sarah was still unsure as to the source of that power. What she did know, was that having the crystal reminded her of Mia's story and her courage, and served to bolster her own strength.

"I was so happy to get your call," Mia said, plunking herself down in front of Sarah.

"I've been thinking a lot about you since that day you walked out of the social services agency. Any second thoughts?"

"Second thoughts, third thoughts. I wouldn't be me if I didn't overthink every decision I make. But I'm done for now, and what feels so good is that the stress that goes with that kind of unrelenting analysis has let up."

"I was jealous of you for just that reason. Stepping out of your head. That has to feel good."

Mia nodded. "So how are *you*?" she asked.

"Good," Sarah said, a lilt in her voice. "I went back to work, which is a good thing, and I'm able to think about something other than me. I really needed to get outside of myself.

"I don't even know what you do," Mia said.

"That's true. You and I kind of skipped over all of that pre-liminary stuff, didn't we? I'm a nurse. I work with cancer patients. I know that a lot of people think that's depressing," she added quickly, as if expecting a reaction from Mia, "but it's just the opposite. It's inspiring to see the resilience of people when they face mortality. What do you do?"

"I'm a health journalist, so I can completely relate to what you're saying. The people I interview give me a healthy dose of per-spective. In fact, well, not to change the subject, but maybe you could help me out."

"Anything," Sarah said, eager to do something for Mia.

"I'm writing a series of articles on living with cancer. I have to fine-tune my angle, but I'm really interested in how people who have cancer think differently about things after their diagnosis or after their treatment or even midway through their treatment. How does it shape who they are as they move forward? Does the disease become part of their identity? Does it haunt them? Or maybe they don't think differently at all about their lives. Maybe for some, cancer is just a detour, and once back on track they leave it as far behind them as possible. You know, questions like that. Do you know anyone who might be willing to talk to me?"

Sarah was mentally going through her patients. Not just any-one would want to talk to a journalist about so personal an experi-ence, but she knew that she could come up with someone.

"Let me think about it," she said. "I'm sure that I'll be able to help you."

"Great. So, you were saying. You went back to work and—"

"And..." Her voice trailed off as she searched for the right words. "And something seems to be changing. It's just like you said, Mia. It's a process, and gradually, without any kind of defining moment something clicks, and I feel like I'm being led to a place that feels right. You said that you feel it in your gut and I think that's what may be happening."

"That's exciting. Tell me about it."

"It's hard to explain, really. It's almost intangible, but I just started to feel different. I don't know. Maggie recently asked me... Maggie's my therapist," Sarah explained and then paused. The only other people who knew that she was seeing a therapist were Matthew and her sister. She had kept it to herself mainly because she thought it would set off her mother in some way and she didn't want to have to deal with that.

"Forget it," Mia said with a wave of her hand, "everyone and their mother are in therapy."

Sarah laughed and continued. "She asked me if I wanted to be pregnant or if I wanted to have a baby. The question really bugged me at the time, but I couldn't stop thinking about it." Mia was nodding, staring at Sarah wide-eyed and hanging onto every word. "Every day I see patients come to the hospital for treatment," Sarah continued. "Some come with friends, some with family, some come alone. And I started thinking about friendship. And I thought, friendship is so special because we choose our friends, we choose them because we like them, because we respect them. And then there are the patients who come with one of their kids, or their husband or wife. Sometimes you can see the love in those relationships and sometimes it's clear that those people are there only because they feel like they have to be there. Then there are those who come alone, even though they do have family members."

"That's so sad," Mia interrupted, "It must break your heart."

"It does. And in those cases, the genetic bond doesn't mean a thing. So, what makes a relationship strong and healthy and meaningful?"

Mia waited for the great revelation but Sarah stopped short

as if stumped by her own question.

"Whatever it is," Sarah finally said, "it's not blood. Besides which, I *was* pregnant. Several times. Didn't turn out so well. So yes, I just want a baby, but more than that, what I really want is to be a parent."

"What's the difference?" Mia asked.

"I'm sure that my kid will give me a lot of happiness. And probably torment me and drive me insane," Sarah quickly added. "But it's not just about what a baby will bring me. I really do believe that I have a lot to give. So does Matthew. I can offer love, I can nurture a child, I can provide a safe place for a kid to grow up, I can be there when life gives him or her a swift kick in the ass. That's what I want. And if I give it to someone who doesn't have my genes, then so be it. This way, I get to give it to someone who really needs it. Hell, just a few minutes ago I even felt a maternal yearning for Jason Destructo."

"Who?"

"Never mind, just some kid."

Sarah herself was surprised at how resolute she sounded. Minutes earlier she had said to Mia that she was starting to feel different, and now as she listened to herself she sounded like a woman on a mission. She had not said one word that was not true. And she was beginning to feel the soothing relief that Mia had experienced.

"So, what now?"

"First, I let my husband in on the news," Sarah said, grinning. "And then, I guess we do what we have to do, as daunting as it may seem." She took the crystal from her pocket and laid it on the table. "It was so generous of you to share this with me. There was something special about having it. It sounds corny, but I drew from your strength."

"It's not corny at all. Though, I'm not sure that it was strength that came up for me that day."

"Sure seemed like it. I'd like you to take your necklace back."

Mia picked it up and looked at it.

"This brings me back to that day when I walked aimlessly and alone in Prague. It feels like a lifetime ago. It was a difficult day, but a great one too." She cocked her head. "You know what? Keep it," she said, sliding it back across the table. "And pass it along to someone else if that seems right. We're building a story with this crystal. Tell it. And maybe the next person will draw upon whatever you whispered to it to find her way through a challenging time."

Sarah felt her skin tingle. Her first instinct was to refuse, but it was exciting to think that she could play a part in what Mia was suggesting. She took the necklace from Mia's hand and slid it back into her jacket pocket.

The next decision was almost as agonizing as the first. Sarah had finally committed to adoption, but whether to adopt locally or internationally was a choice that both she and Matthew struggled with for weeks. Sarah cringed at her mother's insistence on domestic adoption, so the baby wouldn't look like he was adopted. She felt uncomfortable when her sister raised the high costs of adopting a child internationally. That her child might be branded before being able to talk, or chosen because she was a cheaper alternative were thoughts that Sarah aired only with Maggie. She realized that she and Matthew were going to have to be brutally honest about their needs, no matter how ugly.

"Let's make a list. Domestic versus international. Pros and cons," Matthew said over dinner.

"Pros and cons?" Sarah was appalled. "We're talking about a person here."

"Come on, Sarah," he said, going over to the kitchen counter to grab a pen and a piece of paper. "It was your therapist who said we had to be brutally honest."

The list of disadvantages to adopting internationally was long: 1. It was expensive, very expensive; 2. They could not adopt a newborn; 3. There would be uncertainty regarding health issues; 4. They might have to travel to the country of origin for several weeks; 5. Their child would be from another culture and might face racism. On the plus side, the waiting time was significantly shorter than if they adopted locally and they could start their family sooner.

When they were done, Matthew slid the list across the table to Sarah. There were two disadvantages to adopting locally. The first was that they might have to wait for years. They were both young, and though they were eager to grow their family, they were willing to wait. The second disadvantage on the list was tougher. She took the pen from Matthew's hand and underlined it, once, then twice and then three times. In the end, this would be the deciding factor. Sarah looked up at him and without another word the message had been sent and received. A local birth mother could change her mind within thirty days. No matter how remote the possibility, she simply could not take that chance.

With that decision made, Sarah and Matthew visited several agencies, each one designated to manage adoptions for one specific country. Sarah was soon feeling the effects of information overload.

"How are we ever going to choose the country?" she asked Matthew as they lay in bed together. He didn't answer right away and Sarah thought he might have fallen asleep. "Matthew, are you awake?"

"I'm awake." He paused. "What if I were to tell you that I have this image in my head of what our child looks like. I feel like I can see her. I've got this sense of where she's from."

"She? Really?"

"We've done our homework. We've gathered more information than we can possibly absorb. We were able to eliminate a few options on the basis of that information and now it seems like we've reached an impasse because there's nothing more to guide us. So what's going to help us decide? I have this gut feeling, Sarah."

She looked up sharply. "Well, could you share it with me?"

"She's a beautiful baby girl. Well, probably a girl. From China."

"She is?" Sarah whispered, feeling goose bumps rising on her arms. "But—"

"But what?"

Sarah didn't know. She seemed to have no objection though she had become so used to challenging any idea or suggestion. Neither of them spoke. That night, for the first time in a long time, Sarah sank into a restful sleep.

The next day, the peace evaporated. When Matthew arrived home from work insisting they go out for a celebratory dinner, she shook her head. The thought of the pale blue walls in the room upstairs next to theirs seemed unbearable.

"It's too soon."

"Why wait any longer? Sarah, the only thing between us and our child is time. That's it. We still have a long road ahead of us, but we've also travelled a long way. I, for one, will drink to that!"

Standing before her in their kitchen, Matthew was like an eager child himself, his excitement overflowing. She wanted so badly to share it. She deserved it. But more importantly, Matthew deserved it. When she thought about the number of times in the past months that she had pushed him away or blamed him for what he seemed unable to understand, she felt ashamed. And so, with a nod and a hint of a smile, she went upstairs to change.

On the way to her room, Sarah stopped in front of the door that had been kept closed for months now. She placed her hand on the knob, turned it and pushed. The emptiness of the room made her feel sick. Physically sick. *We will have to paint in here,* she thought and backed slowly out of the room.

In her own bedroom, Sarah sat on the edge of the bed and felt her body return to normal. Tonight would be about her and Matthew having an evening out, nothing more. She slipped on a dress Matthew was fond of, freshened up her makeup and slid into a black pair of high-heeled sandals that killed her feet and back. As if ceremoniously adding the final touch, she opened the lid of her jewellery box and pulled out Mia's necklace, securing it around her neck and then heading back down the stairs to join her husband.

CHAPTER 23
KATE

It was a moment where there was no sound, no movement, and no light. It was a moment imbued with a paralyzing fear. Kate sat upright in bed, beads of sweat beginning to trickle down her face. Something felt different. Something felt strange. Slowly, she slid her hand up under her pyjama top and touched her left breast. Gently at first, and then with more pressure. It was unmistakeable. There was something there. Kate only realized she had been gasping for air when Daniel stirred and turned over.

"What's wrong?" he asked, his voice raspy with sleep.

"I don't know! It's just, I think—" She barely recognized her own voice. There was a sense of panic that she had never heard before. Not after her diagnosis. Not before surgery. Not during her chemotherapy treatment. Through the worst of it, Kate had not broken. There had been moments to navigate with Zoë, issues to resolve with Daniel, and times when she felt the life draining from her. But even as she lay curled up on the bathroom floor, she had remained steady in her determination.

"What is it?" Daniel sat up.

"I feel something, it doesn't feel right. I think it's a lump. But that's not possible. I just finished chemo. I... I'm done. I did what I was supposed to do. I got through it. How can this be?"

"Okay, don't panic," Daniel said, turning on the lamp beside the bed.

Kate jumped out of bed. "Don't panic? Are you out of your fucking mind? How the hell can you say that? Have you not been here for the past four months? Have you not seen what I've been through? What if I have to do it all again?"

She began to cry. Daniel took her shaking body in his arms until eventually she lay still. "I'm just not that strong," she whimpered. "I'm just not that strong."

"Yes, you are." His grip on her tightened. "Maybe you're getting a bit ahead of yourself. Maybe what you felt is nothing at all. Just because you got it once doesn't mean you'll get it again. We'll call the doctor on Monday." He stood up slowly, bringing Kate with him and led her back to the bed. Like a frightened child, she pulled the covers up to her chin and turned her face toward him as he bent over and kissed her forehead.

Though she tried to will herself to sleep, her mind had already begun an unstoppable descent into fear and hopelessness. Since her diagnosis, Kate had used every bit of energy she had to fight the undertow. Every day that she stepped into that hospital she had seen people around her get sucked into a vortex of despair. Some tried to free themselves, while others succumbed to a power greater than their own. But Kate, as always, had kept her head level.

As she lay in bed, she wondered why a rational person like herself was unravelling now. She tried to talk herself out of the terror that gripped her, and replayed what Daniel had said to her just minutes earlier. *I'm panicking for no reason.* She resisted the temptation to touch her breast again, knowing that it would likely feed her fear. But even as she felt her heart rate slow she understood that cancer would always be part of her life, even if she got through it this time. It's a life sentence. Every ache, every pain, every lump, every bump will be reason to think that it's back.

The questions assailed her like rapid machine-gun fire. She placed her hands over her ears to stop them. She recognized that she was mapping out her future, filling it with worry and uncertainty. But she couldn't stop the machinations. Kate was starting to feel exhausted from all the mental gymnastics but sleep still eluded her. She tried to imagine what Angel might say. *Baby steps, Kate.* Daniel was snoring softly beside her and the sight of his tranquil face unnerved her more. How could he sleep while she agonized?

During her first meeting with Angel, the nurse had suggested seeking help through support groups. Kate had dismissed the idea, uncomfortable with the thought of sharing the intimate details of her experience with people she didn't know. Plus, she didn't want to give the cancer more space than it was already occupying. Besides, she didn't believe that she needed it. She thought that she had plenty of support. But, as it turned out, her family couldn't provide what she needed. Sophie was always there for her. She showed genuine concern and often offered to come with her to treatments or to cook meals. Other friends tried to do and say the right thing. Her parents suffered alongside her, trying to be brave. But despite a strong entourage, Kate often felt empty, with her needs unmet. It wasn't their fault. She herself couldn't pinpoint what it was that she needed. Only someone who had been in her shoes, who had endured debilitating nausea, collapsed veins, hair loss and all the rest could truly understand. Those people could not only say the words she needed to hear, but they knew what they were.

She tried to summon the pragmatic Kate. She always felt better when she had a plan, though cancer seemed to take plans and mangle them. While she could count on reason in most areas of life, it seemed to be failing her now.

Kate came back to her breath. Before Kate began her treatments, Angel had told her how deep breathing or meditation could help reduce her stress. She never really tried it until now, inhaling and exhaling deeply. The sound of her breath, the low rumble coming from Daniel, and the faint din of the early morning traffic joined in a cadenced rhythm, and lulled her, finally, to sleep.

CHAPTER 24
SOPHIE

The ringing phone awakened her. Sophie squinted to see the clock. It was 7 a.m. When she answered the phone she could barely hear the person on the other end of the line and had to ask who it was. "Kate? My goodness, you sound awful. What's wrong?"

"I'm sure it's nothing. Did I wake you? What time is it?"

Sophie had become used to being the caller. She phoned often, sometimes to check up on her friend, sometimes to talk about herself. Instinct told her that this call probably wasn't nothing.

"What's going on?"

"I felt something, kind of, I don't know, weird. I'm worried that maybe—"

"I'm sure you're right. It's probably nothing." But even as the words left her lips, Sophie was doubting. If she were Kate, she would think exactly what Kate was thinking. "You'll just do what you've done so far. Get it checked out and deal with whatever it is with the same grace and determination that you've shown until now."

Kate had often been a mother figure to Sophie given their fifteen-year age gap and Sophie seldom found herself in the role of nurturer in the relationship.

"I'll see my doctor this week and we'll take it from there."

"This week? Why not today? Why not right now?"

"It doesn't work like that."

Sophie heard Jessie's bedroom door open and the door to the bathroom close seconds later. "What can I do? Do you want me to come with you?"

"No, thanks. Daniel said he'd go. Sophie, I swear, I damn near lost it this time. I don't know what came over me. I've maintained control until now, but I went crazy."

"You can't keep it together all the time. I would have gone to pieces immediately and a million times over." Sophie sat upright and swung her legs over the side of the bed.

"So. What's new with you?" Kate asked.

Sophie hesitated, thrown by the abrupt change of subject. "Kate. Seriously?"

"Yes. Seriously. I have to busy my mind otherwise I'll go insane." Kate sounded more like herself again. Her voice was a little stronger. Sophie was reluctant to speak about herself, but Kate persisted. Maybe it was what she needed right now. "How's school going? How are the kids? How's Alex?"

"Great, fine, and I have no idea. He's in Florida. Again."

"What's he doing in Florida?"

"He says that he has a client there."

"What do you mean he *says* that he has a client? You don't believe him?"

"I don't know what to think anymore. I just have no idea how we got here."

"I have news for you, Sophie. You were always here. You just didn't notice or you didn't care." Even in a weakened state, Kate could still wield sharp words, oblivious of their effect.

"Listen Kate, I'm happy to talk to you about what you're going through, but if you'd rather not, I understand." It came out more brusquely than she had intended. "Give me a call if you need me. And please let me know as soon as you've seen your doctor."

"Oh." Kate sounded surprised. "Of course. I'll talk to you soon."

As Sophie hung up the phone she felt a rush of both guilt and anger. Her friend needed her, she knew, and she regretted ending their conversation so abruptly. She felt sympathy for what Kate was facing and wanted to be a good friend to her. But today she lost patience. Usually she excused Kate's blunt assessments of her marriage, believing her friend had her best interest at heart. But today she resented the judgments she cast.

Sophie should have known that Kate would be all over her if she insinuated that Alex was doing something other than work in Florida. The truth was, Sophie had no reason to believe that Alex was up to anything. Despite his not-so-subtle efforts to sabotage her newfound interests, she trusted him. And if she weren't constantly defying him, he wouldn't be so belligerent. She didn't know why she was always rebelling. Stranger still, the thought of his cheating on her was not devastating. It's not like she didn't care, and it's not like she wouldn't be hurt and angry by the betrayal, but it would almost be easier. Then she would know what to do. And frankly, it would ease her conscience.

Kate would support her if ever she chose to leave Alex. But not everyone in her circle would. Not everyone disapproved of Alex which, while infuriating to Kate, was also validating. Her parents thought Alex could do no wrong. When Sophie expressed even a mild complaint about his frequent absences, her father sprang to his defence, reminding her that he was doing what he needed to do to support his family. And when she told her mother that Alex did not want her to pursue her own interests, she too dismissed Sophie's desires as being secondary to the marriage. Sophie wasn't particularly surprised by any of this. Each day of her parents' forty-year marriage was reminiscent of those old television shows, with the mother clad in an apron she never took off, tending to every last whim of her man. It was times like these that Sophie wished she hadn't been an only child.

Sophie found herself suspended somewhere between Kate's uncompromising stance and her parents' categorical acceptance of whatever Alex did. She waffled daily, tending towards one extreme and then the other. In the face of Kate's indictments she would be more defensive of Alex while her parents' inability to expand their minds could launch her into a ten minute diatribe about her own desires and how Alex couldn't care less about them.

Tensions between Alex and Sophie had never been higher. He was away a lot, and when he was home he parked himself in front of the television. The absent-father deal was bad for their kids. Jessie was now a self-absorbed teen, but Gabe missed his dad, though he didn't complain.

"Why don't you spend a bit of time with your son?" she had asked Alex the week before. "You're away so much."

"I'm not lying on a beach, Sophie. I'm working." But then he softened. "I'll do something with Gabe this weekend. I promise."

Despite their crumbling relationship, the idea of living alone scared her. She had never been on her own. She had gone from her parents' house to her husband's. Now Alex was often not around which meant that she spent many evenings solo. So she was only too happy to accept a classmate's invitation to go for a drink after class one evening.

◆

Peter had rescued her on the night of her first class when he found her walking through the labyrinth of corridors, looking lost. Sophie had been embarrassed, admitting that it had been years since she had last been at the university.

"You realize, that I'm about a dozen years older than you, don't you?" she had asked as they sat down at the bar. "And I'm married."

"Uh, okay," Peter stammered. "I figured you were married because of the ring, but I have to say I didn't really think about your age."

Sophie covered her eyes with her hand. "I'm sorry. That's so presumptuous. You must think I'm the biggest idiot."

"You're not an idiot."

When she got home that night and the babysitter told her that Alex had called looking for her, she smiled. When she called him back, she didn't mean to tell him where she had been. Not that she wanted to hide it, but she knew he wouldn't like it. Despite everything, she didn't want to upset him. But he persisted.

Didn't we agree that you would come right home after class? It's a long time for the kids to be alone," Alex said.

"I had a quick drink with a classmate. And we had no such agreement. Secondly, they're not alone. Was there anything else?"

"A male classmate?"

"Yes, Alex, a male classmate. What difference does it make?"

"Well, I just wanted to check up on my wife and children, but I guess you're managing to fill your time."

Had she not spent the previous two hours engaged in conversation with someone who appeared genuinely interested in her, who shared her love of art, and who didn't belittle her, Sophie probably would not have noticed the sarcasm. As she hung up the phone, she felt her chest constrict, feeling resentment and guilt in equal measure.

Could she be blamed for turning to someone else? Who wouldn't understand why she would be drawn to another person who recognized her value? Besides which, it had only been a harmless kiss. With that thought, her stomach lurched. She grabbed the phone, dialled Alex again, but hung up before the first ring, because she had no idea what she would say when he answered.

CHAPTER 25

KATE

"**G**o home, Kate."

Kate barely moved.

"Go home," he repeated. "It's nothing."

Kate could feel Daniel's gaze as they both digested what the doctor had just said but she could look neither at Daniel nor at the doctor sitting behind his desk. Instead, she stared blankly at the stapler, which sat upon it. She waited for relief to register, but she had been so overwrought that she still felt as if an eighteen-wheeler had flattened her.

"Kate? That's great news," Daniel said. "Isn't it?"

"But there was something there," she insisted.

"Yes. But it's not cancer. You're fine," he said, scanning the mammogram report.

"How can you be sure?" Kate mumbled. "Don't you want to do a biopsy just to be sure?"

"I *am* sure, Kate. It's nothing to worry about. You can go ahead and start your radiation as planned."

"Kate, let's go. This is what we wanted to hear," Daniel said, standing up. He tugged gently at her arm. "I don't understand," he said to her once they had left the doctor's office. "I would have thought you'd be jumping for joy. You look like you just got terrible news."

"I know it's good news. I just... I don't know. I still feel so... It's weird." Kate walked over to a bench and sat down. She looked up at Daniel. "You probably have so much work to do. I know you cancelled appointments this week. Why don't you go ahead? I'll walk home."

"Kate, it'll take you at least an hour to walk. Let me drive you home."

"I want to walk. Really. If I get tired I'll flag a taxi."

Daniel sat down beside her. Kate knew that he always wanted to do and say the right thing and in this case he needed to be coaxed to do what instinct told him he shouldn't.

"I don't feel right leaving you," he said.

As he got up and walked away, Kate saw him look back at her. She would berate herself later for having accused him of not being present with her and then dismissing him when he was. But her thoughts quickly returned to herself. None of this made any sense. She had shown such resilience in the past few months. She was the first to deliver a morbid joke, shocking her friends. And from what the doctor told her, she was through the worst of it, with radiation therapy lying between her and a return to normalcy. But at this moment she felt sadder than she had felt since her diagnosis. Normal did not seem possible.

"Kate?" She looked up, startled. "It's Sarah. Angel."

"Oh, hi."

Angel hesitated, then sat down on the bench. "Are you all right?"

"I just had an appointment with my doctor. I thought there was something to worry about but I just learned that there isn't."

"And yet, there's no joy."

Kate shook her head.

"And you're thinking that there must be something wrong with you for feeling this way." Kate was nodding now.

Angel glanced at her watch.

"I don't want to keep you," Kate said. "Please don't worry about me. I'll be fine."

"No, it's not that. I was just wondering if there might be a support group starting soon. Remember we talked about that?"

"I don't know. I'm just not that comfortable with—"

"Walk with me," Angel said as she stood. "It's just one floor up. I'm not even sure that there's a group right now." She extended an arm toward Kate.

Two minutes later Kate found herself waiting in an empty room for a women's support group which would begin in fifteen minutes. Once again, Angel sat down beside her and Kate wondered if she planned on staying. "No one but you could have gotten me in here," she said, and smiled for the first time in over a week. Angel looked as if she was about to say something but then sat back, reconsidering.

"I know how isolated and lonely you can feel when you're going through something like this. Not everyone can understand." Kate remembered their last encounter and wondered if Angel was talking from personal experience. "Your husband mentioned to me that I had been helpful to you, even when I wasn't here." It wasn't a question but Kate sensed that Angel was waiting for a response.

"You were. You make me want to fight harder," Kate said. "You're a real comfort. Which is kind of strange," she continued, "since you left so soon after we met to go on maternity—." Angel looked stricken. "I've upset you. I wasn't thinking. I'm so—"

"I was just thinking about someone I met recently who had the same impact on me as I seem to have had on you. She was facing a challenge and I was touched by her. I admired the way she embraced the unknown. She was scared, but she still walked toward it. I felt strengthened after I met her even though she was a stranger. So what you're saying makes perfect sense to me."

Angel reached into her pocket and pulled out a necklace.

"The woman gave this crystal to me. She said it recalled a time in her life when she felt strong and resolved. When I look at it I think of her and how she finally found her peace. Sometimes, when you're dealing with something that is so difficult, regardless of what it is, it's helpful to know that others go through hardships too and that they come out on the other side and are often better for it. So, please take this necklace and let it be a reminder that you can face whatever life brings. And then, when you like, offer it to someone else who needs it."

Kate couldn't speak for a second. "Don't you need it?" she asked, when she could open her mouth.

"Not anymore," Angel said, as if just now coming to this realization. Neither of them spoke for a full minute. But then the silence was broken by the loud chatter of two women walking into the room. Kate barely noticed them or that Angel had stood up. She was mesmerized, rubbing her fingers over the face of the crystal, inspecting the links of the silver chain. When she looked up, Angel was moving toward the door. She waved and disappeared from view.

Kate turned toward the two women who had taken their seats across from her in the small circle of chairs.

"I'm Michelle," one of them said, offering her hand.

"Paula," the second woman said, following Michelle's lead.

"I'm Kate," she said. "This is my first time here."

Michelle was close to her age, in her fifties. Paula was in her forties. Mary, the fourth woman in the group, was in her seventies. Each of them was at a different stage of treatment and each had a story to tell. She felt at ease and was surprised to hear herself sharing details about her own treatment, her family, her friends and her latest collapse after months of brittle control. As she told her story, the women nodded. Michelle chimed in with, "I felt exactly the same way." There was no "it could be so much worse" or "just count your blessings that you actually have a husband who cares." There was no judgment or disbelief when she told them about her recent results and the lack of elation. Instead, there was understanding. No matter what the outcome, cancer had changed her forever. They got it.

During the first session, Kate learned something from every one of them even though their experiences had been so different from hers. Paula had completed her treatment and was happy to report her NED status. Kate waited, hoping someone else would ask for a translation.

"Your what status?" she finally asked. "I guess I'm not up on the lingo."

"NED," Paula answered. "No evidence of disease."

"That's wonderful," Kate said, but immediately wished she hadn't.

"It is, of course it is." There was hesitation in Paula's voice, even though the words were positive. "I have gone through a diagnosis, surgery and treatment and only now am I coming to a group. Because I kind of feel like you did, Kate. 'Everything looks good. Get on with living.' That's what every doctor has said. But I can't seem to do it yet. I'm afraid to not be afraid. If I relax, I can't help feeling something awful will happen." The words were fraught with weariness and Kate could feel Paula's exhaustion.

"I would guess," said Michelle, "that with a bit of time it will become easier to relax and to live normally again. I'm hoping, anyway. Personally, I can't wait until I don't have to think about it every day."

Michelle had lymphoma and was in the middle of chemo treatment. She was divorced, had no children, was an only child, and both her parents had died within the past five years. She said that she had some friends but, like Kate, she felt that they often didn't know quite what to do or say and some even chose to stay away. Usually, Michelle went to chemo sessions on her own. The one time that she brought a friend with her, she spent most of her time worrying about her friend and making sure that she wasn't uncomfortable. Everyone in the group had felt alone and afraid at some point, but Michelle's fears were particularly dark. The worst one was that she would die at home and no one would know.

"I know it sounds crazy, but it could be days or weeks before someone found me."

"I'll check in with you, Michelle. Every day," Kate said. Her response felt completely natural.

Michelle laughed. "Seriously? For the rest of my life?"

"Sure. Whatever. Until you feel secure again." Kate felt great making this small gesture and could now see the value of connecting with others in this way. "I went to a lecture recently and the woman who spoke was also single. Her name was Erica something."

The group facilitator, Hannah, interjected. "Erica Dunham. She'd be a great person to speak with, Michelle. There are support groups for people living solo with cancer. You don't have to go through this alone." Michelle's face relaxed a little and Kate was happy that somehow she had played a role, however small, in that transition.

Mary was seventy-nine and feisty. It was her second time facing cancer and she was admirably defiant. When Mary railed against those "wanker doctors" who told her to take comfort in the fact that she had lived a long, fulfilling life, Kate laughed at her acerbic tongue. Though she had emigrated to Canada years ago, she had kept her thick Irish accent.

"I mean, Jaysus," Mary continued, "those lads have got me dead and buried long before I've taken my last breath. And their endless questions. I've got a mind to tell them to ask my arse!"

Everyone enjoyed Mary's rants, which she did without apology or particular consideration for those she might offend. Kate and the others appreciated all that had been done for them by the doctors and nurses and they knew that they owed their lives to what could only be considered as heroic acts by their medical professionals. But each of them also had anecdotes of shocking things that some doctors had said or done. Mary was their voice.

Mary was somewhat more sensitive toward her fellow cancer patients but remained forthright. When Paula complained that she was afraid of being happy, Mary leaned forward in her chair and wagged her finger. "Now don't you go wasting one more day. If it's a good day, then enjoy it. No one knows what the future holds, dear. With or without cancer. If you live your life worrying, you might as well be dead." Kate looked at Paula, who was stunned by what sounded like an admonishment. But the women quickly learned to appreciate Mary and realize that her words, despite their delivery, were wise. Had Daniel expressed the very same thought, Kate would have dismissed it as a platitude from someone who did not know the realities of disease. Coming from Mary, the sentiment resonated.

Kate was taken by surprise when, after the meeting, Michelle asked if she would like to go to a movie. Kate narrowed her eyes; she didn't know when she had last seen a movie and was hard-pressed to remember when she had gone out alone with one of her women friends. She hesitated, but could not find a reason to turn down the invitation. In fact, she didn't want to find a reason.

That night, Kate indulged. She nestled into the oversized movie theatre seat, sipped a massive soda and plunged her hand into a jumbo bucket of buttery popcorn.

As she waited in the dark for the movie to start, Kate opened her purse and unzipped the inside pocket. Even in darkness she could see the glimmer of the crystal that Angel had given her. She leaned back in her seat, Michelle by her side, and felt safe for the first time in months. These newfound friends would be, she was certain, life-sustaining.

CHAPTER 26
SOPHIE

There was nothing innocent about it. Sophie was now wracked with guilt.

The week that Alex got back from Florida, Sophie skipped her class and cooked an elaborate three-course dinner for him and the kids. She joined him for a business dinner one night and the following night the two of them danced together at a cancer research benefit. The guilt receded. They even laughed together. The previous Sunday, when Sophie suggested that they all head out to a movie together, Alex and Gabe jumped at the idea. Even Jessie emerged from her room to join them.

This week, however, when she reminded him that she would be out for the evening, he asked, "Are you still doing that?" as if she was engaging in illicit behaviour.

The tension that had dissipated over the past two weeks began to mount again. Sophie wondered if placing her own needs and desires before her husband's was really worth it. Maybe she was being the selfish one, jeopardizing their family life. "I don't have to go tonight if there's something else you'd rather do," she said compliantly.

"Great," he said, but offered nothing else.

After dinner, Alex retreated to his study. Sophie sat in front of the TV by herself. When the phone rang, she ran for it.

A man's voice said her name.

"Who is this?"

"Peter." Sophie felt her face flush. She didn't remember giving him her phone number.

"How did you get my number? Why are you calling?" she whispered.

"You weren't in class tonight. Or last week. I was worried."

"I'm fine. Just taking a break."

"A break? That's not really how it works, Sophie. Maybe you've forgotten, seeing as how it's been so long for you. In university, *they* tell you when you can take a break," he teased.

Sophie wasn't feeling particularly playful. "My husband's home! He could've answered the phone!"

"It's not like we're having an affair. I'm just some guy in your class, calling to check up on you. That's all."

"You kissed me!" Sophie said, as if she was the innocent victim.

"I know, I know. I'm sorry. But I think you kissed me back."

There, he said it. Sophie had replayed the incident in her mind countless times. She had withdrawn from him immediately, hadn't she? She put her hand to her forehead and felt the heat and perspiration.

"Let's just forget about it," Peter said.

"I have to focus on my family right now." During the two hours that she and Peter had spent chatting, she'd mentioned Alex's opposition to the class.

"Is something wrong?" he asked.

"Everything's fine, we just—"

"I just don't want you to stay away from class because of me."

"You're not the reason," she lied. "Besides which, Alex is probably right. How is this class going to help me anyway? And for the past two weeks things have been peaceful around here. Peace is worth a lot in my books."

"How come things can't be peaceful even if you're going to school? You seemed to be enjoying the class, is all I'm saying. It would be a shame to give it up." It was what Kate would say. "Anyway, I should let you go. I hope you come back." There was a click as Peter hung up.

Was this focusing on her family? She was sitting alone in her den while Alex was in his study and the kids were holed up in their rooms. Just then, the two of them came bounding down the stairs. Gabe flung himself onto the sofa beside Sophie and Jessie plopped down in the leather high back chair.

"I'm hungry," Gabe complained.

"So what else is new? Go get yourself a snack." Sophie said.

"I'm tired." He obeyed her, though, hoisting himself up from the sofa and trotting off toward the kitchen.

Jessie was slumped in the chair examining her fingernails. "What's doing, Jess?"

"Nothing. Didn't you have school tonight?"

"I decided not to go."

"Why?" Even Jessie was accusatory.

"Didn't have the energy."

"Tonight, last week. I thought you liked it."

"I did. I do."

"It's because of Dad, isn't it? He doesn't want you to go, so you don't."

"I needed a break," she said, even though Peter had just rejected the excuse. "But it has been nice around here, don't you think?"

"Whatever." Jessie picked up the remote and flipped on the TV. Sophie frowned.

"Are you mad or something?" Sophie asked.

"I'm not mad. I just think it's kind of lame. You finally decide to do something for yourself and then you quit."

"I didn't quit." Sophie was surprised that Jessie had even formed an opinion on the subject.

"'You have to follow through with your commitments, Jess.' That's what you're always telling me. Why should I believe you when you tell me that I can do anything that I want in life? That what's most important is that I'm happy and that I do it because I want to and not because of what anyone else thinks?" Having finished her rant, Jessie turned up the volume on the television.

Sophie felt sick. Here she was trying to keep the peace in her family and was now being called out by a veritable stranger and by her thirteen-year-old daughter. But as she thought of Alex, barricaded upstairs behind a closed door, heat flushed her face.

"Jessie, turn the TV down!" she barked.

Jessie clicked off the television altogether. She stood and ran up the stairs to her room, closing yet another door on Sophie.

CHAPTER 27

KATE

K ate was surprised to find Angel waiting for her as she left her support group meeting. Since Angel had passed along the crystal to her a few weeks earlier, Kate had thought of her – and thanked her – every day. It didn't take long for Kate to realize how vital connecting with these women would be. Finally, someone understood her. Finally, she did not have to worry about what she said and how it would be received. Kate had begun to feel like herself again and life with her family was getting back on track. Cancer had changed her. A lot. She had learned that from her group meetings. But Daniel and the kids still got back the wife and mother they knew and had temporarily lost.

Kate was still going for radiation but compared to chemo, it was a cakewalk. She was tired a lot of the time but that was the worst of it. The uncertainty of what lay ahead still crept up on her, paralyzing her if she let it. Instead, she reached into her purse and felt the smooth surface of the crystal. She also recited Mary's words in her head like a mantra: "No one knows what the future holds. With or without cancer. If you live your life worrying, you might as well be dead."

"Kate, can I talk to you for a moment?" Angel asked. Angel guided her to the chairs in the waiting room. A cold sweat broke on the back of her neck though she knew that Angel couldn't be bringing bad news. As they sat down, Kate noticed that Angel seemed a bit uneasy.

"Is anything wrong?" Kate asked.

"Oh, no. Sorry. I didn't mean to make you nervous. Nothing is wrong. Nothing at all."

"Looks like I'm still on high alert for bad news," Kate said. She let out a small sigh.

"That'll go away in time. Listen, a friend of mine is a journalist and she's doing a piece on people who have cancer, or who have had cancer, and how it has changed them. I know this is a bit awkward but I think you would be the perfect person for her to interview."

"Talk to a journalist? Well, I suppose I could—" Kate didn't complete her thought. Angel had been so helpful to her that she couldn't imagine saying no to any simple request. On the other hand, could she really tell a reporter what it's been like for her? She was just beginning to feel comfortable talking within the safe confines of a support group.

Angel filled the silence as Kate considered the idea. "It might interest you to know that this journalist, Mia, was the person who gave me the crystal pendant which I passed on to you." Ever since Angel had given her the necklace, Kate had conjured up all sorts of stories about its previous owner. She assumed that Angel's recent loss had something to do with why she had clung to it and she wondered why she had been ready to give it up.

"I often think about where that crystal came from and how it made its way to me. How did you know that you were ready to give it up?" Kate wanted an answer to the question but she was also trying to find out what lay beneath Angel's confident smile today.

"Well," said Angel after a pause, "I realized I wasn't afraid of all the unanswered questions."

"So there are still unanswered questions?" Kate asked, dismayed.

"Yes. But I'm okay with that. Correction: I'm a little better with it."

"Does this have anything to do with your having a family?" Kate asked. People said she often overstepped boundaries, but Angel's gesture had been so personal that Kate gave herself permission to try and learn more about how this person she so admired had faced her own challenges. She guessed she'd gone too far when Angel's face flushed. "It's none of my business, I know. And our relationship is supposed to be purely professional—"

"No, no," said Angel. "It's okay. I don't blame you for wondering. Goodness, you must have thought it was a bit unusual for me to give you this pendant. So I will tell you this. As you know, I did lose my baby. In fact," she continued, "I gave birth to him knowing that he had already died." Kate put her hand over her mouth. Angel forged ahead, not noticing. "My husband and I decided to adopt a baby." Kate knew she was just getting the headlines, but this was fine. "It was a long journey to get there and my husband arrived before I did. But once I caught up to him, it seemed like, or it felt like, the absolute right decision for us."

"That's good news, then," Kate said and Angel nodded. "So now what?"

"Now we wait. We completed a massive amount of paperwork," she said. "And had a visit from the social worker. Now we wait to get the phone call."

"And then?"

"And then we're off to China."

As Kate thought about what Angel just shared, she remembered the day that she arrived for her treatment and found that Angel wasn't there. She had felt abandoned when, really, Angel had been going through a hell of her own. Kate didn't know how Mia fit into

Angel's picture, but she was grateful she'd been there for her.

"What are the unanswered questions?" Kate pressed on.

"There are a ton of them. How long will we have to wait? How will I feel when I meet my child? Will it be an instant bond or will it take time? Will there be health issues? What will it be like to raise a child from a different culture and how will it be for him or her to live in North America? There's still so much that I don't know. But..." Angel trailed off without finishing the thought. "I've talked too much," she said. "I didn't even ask how you are."

"Good. Better. I've met some pretty incredible women here. Did I thank you?"

Angel shook her head as if to say no thanks necessary. "You can tell your friend Mia that I would be happy to talk to her."

CHAPTER 28

SOPHIE

The painting in front of Sophie swirled and flowed with a sort of organized chaos. She took a breath. It was like a mirror image of her own life. On the surface she still played her role and seemed to be in control. Yet beneath the apparent perfection, lay a tangle of doubt and turmoil. She sat down on a bench to rest and saw Peter from the corner of her eye. Her professor and other classmates had left the hall, but she had lingered to enjoy the exhibit in solitude.

"Enjoying?" he asked as he walked up. When she met his gaze, he sat down beside her.

"Very much." She was quiet for a moment, deciding how to proceed. An apology seemed the best course. "I was out of line when we spoke. I'm sorry."

He raised his hand. "No apology required. I shouldn't have offered unsolicited advice. You were right. I hardly know you."

It was what Sophie knew he would say and thought he should say. But it was a disappointment, nonetheless. It was as if the intimacy that she felt on their night out had never happened. But she couldn't have it both ways. She couldn't scold him for being intrusive and get upset when he backed away.

"But I'm glad to see you're back in class."

"I never really left. As I said, I was taking a break to focus on my family. There wasn't ever any question as to whether or not I would come back." Even as she said it, she cringed at her hypocrisy.

"Well. Good." Peter stood up.

"You don't have to go," she said. "I like talking to you. It's easy. I was enjoying the friendship. Up until the time I wigged out on you anyway. But Peter, what happened that night, I realize now was my fault. It can never happen again. Being with Alex isn't exactly blissful right now, but I am married."

"Yeah, I know. I'm pretty sure I wasn't the one who made the first move, Sophie."

She detected irritation in his tone and sighed as the memory of that evening returned. "I know, I know. I take complete responsibility. I'm just saying that it was a mistake."

Sophie knew that she didn't want to be that woman, the woman who allows herself to stray because her husband is self-obsessed. The problem remained, that she didn't know what woman she did want to be. In the past few weeks, Sophie had gone out of her way to be attentive to Alex. Not only had she skipped her classes, but she also made every effort to be available to him whenever he needed her. Twice he asked her to join him for business dinners and she did so willingly. On both occasions, Alex's business associates came alone, their wives obviously having the good sense to stay at home. Though they were perfectly cordial and made some attempt to include Sophie in the conversation, it invariably turned to business and she was left counting the minutes until she could go home. After the second time, Sophie asked Alex why he wanted her there.

"I like you with me. Why? Didn't you have a good time?"

"No, Alex, I didn't have a good time. Couldn't you tell? You didn't talk to me the entire last hour."

"Okay, fine. You don't have to come with me next time."

"Gee, thanks."

"Listen, Sophie. That's not fair. You want to come? Great. You don't want to come? Fine too. What more do you want from me?"

Nothing more, she thought. Just something different. "Maybe we should get some counselling," she had said, changing the subject, and the conversation continued on a path to nowhere. Alex thought her idea was ridiculous, that there was nothing wrong with their marriage, and that even if there was, the two of them were perfectly capable of resolving their problems on their own.

Sophie vacillated. When conversations with Alex left her near apoplectic, an occurrence that was becoming more and more frequent, she was determined and ready to make a drastic move. Alex, she imagined herself saying, I think we need some time apart. The thought of uttering those words left her feeling queasy. What would happen next? And then, fuelled by panic, she could convince herself that she had not fought hard enough – or at all – to repair the relationship and save her family.

Sophie had been keeping Kate at arm's length but she missed having someone to talk to. She phoned to check up on her but remained quiet about her own life.

So that left Peter. She had few other people to turn to. "I had decided not to return to class," Sophie said suddenly. "I probably overreacted to your call because you were right. Looks like you know me better than I gave you credit for," she said.

"So what made you come back?"

"My daughter. She wasn't particularly impressed by my attempts to keep the peace. I thought I was doing the right thing for her. For everyone in my family, really. Without knowing it, by taking an art class I had set an example. You can go after what you want, when you want, despite the obstacles."

"Obstacles?"

"People. Person, rather."

"Smart kid."

"I know," Sophie said with pride. "I didn't want to let her down."

"What about—. Oh, never mind." Peter was treading lightly, not wanting to trespass.

"Say it," Sophie coaxed.

"What about letting yourself down?"

Their professor approached, signalling that they would be leaving soon. Sophie left the question unanswered, which was just as well. But as she drove home that day she ruminated on it. *What about me?* Sophie spent so much time tending to her husband and kids that thinking about herself was almost foreign. Was her marriage more important than her own desires? Was one art class worth giving up what she had at home?

"What the hell do you want?" she yelled, gripping the steering wheel. And with the question asked, finally came the answer, simple, pure and true: "I just want to be happy," she said aloud, relieved, though at a complete loss as to how it could be achieved.

◇

Sophie hadn't known what to expect when she opened her front door. Kate had called that afternoon and asked if she could drop by for a visit and though they still spoke regularly, it had been many weeks since the two had seen one another. Kate's face was drawn and pale but there was a calmness to her.

"Come in. We'll go into the kitchen. Would you like something to drink?"

"No, thank you." They sat opposite one another at the kitchen table. "I joined a support group," she said.

"Great," Sophie said.

"I wanted to say that I'm sorry," Kate said, changing the subject. The apology took Sophie by surprise. Try as she did to be supportive of a friend who was facing the biggest trial of her life, Sophie had withdrawn from Kate. And she felt guilty about it. Then again, she felt guilty about everything these days.

"About what?" Sophie asked cautiously.

"About being a bitch."

Sophie raised her eyebrows.

"I was harsh. No one can really know what it's like to be in someone else's shoes." Kate fidgeted with the strap of her purse. "What I mean is that it's really easy for me to say that Alex treats you like crap and that it's time to think of yourself, but it's probably not that simple."

Sophie stiffened. At the heart of the apology lay a condemnation of her husband. She stood up, turned her back to Kate, and started to scrub the kitchen counter.

"If I had been Daniel on that day that my doctor told me I was okay, I probably would have ranted about how elated I should be, how I have to learn to move on. But he was kind to me. And I wish I'd have been kind like that to you. Shown you the same understanding that people like the women in the support group and you, by the way, have so generously offered me. I thought I was in control, but I was more messed up than I imagined. This group helped me see that."

"Wow," Sophie said. "What's changed?"

"Well, it's not like there's been some sort of metamorphosis. I can't say that I'm free of all fear, but I feel the uncertainty a bit differently. This might sound odd, but thinking about the future caused me more distress than dealing with what was happening in the present. I had cancer. Can I use the past tense yet?" she grinned, not waiting for an answer. "I knew what I had to do and I did it. I dealt with it. But how do you live with not knowing what might come in the next thirty years? The answer to that question wasn't in the brochure."

Sophie leaned in. "How do you deal with uncertainty?" she asked.

"First, I had to accept it, and give up on trying to make the unknown known. No matter what we're living, there's so much that we can't know. Best we can do is just work with whatever comes our way. You have no idea how liberating it was for me to realize that."

Sophie listened closely. The words were true, but they weren't going to solve her own problems. If she stayed with Alex, life would be predictable, not uncertain. She could draw an accurate picture of what things might look like twenty-five years down the road.

"Sounds right," Sophie said quietly. "The main thing is that you're doing well."

"I am. And how are you doing?"

Sophie had promised herself that she would keep talk about herself to a minimum, but given Kate's admission, she had to say something. In truth, Sophie missed talking to Kate.

"I'm okay, I guess. You are harsh about Alex. But you also have a point. He's a good man, a good father. In a lot of ways he's even a good husband. But I'm not happy." Sophie waited for Kate's interjection. It didn't come. She was sitting perfectly still, watching her with warm eyes.

"Things have changed," Sophie said.

"You changed. That's not a bad thing."

"But he hasn't changed with me."

Kate paused, clearly trying to find the right words. "He doesn't have to change. But he does have to accept changes in you. Don't you think so?" Sophie did not have the answers, but apparently Kate did not seem to mind. She moved on. "You once mentioned that you had a contact at an art gallery downtown."

"Oh, that. I actually kind of forgot about it. Going back to school seemed to be enough for now."

"Baby steps," Kate said.

"Kate, what should I do?" Sophie asked, even though she had vowed not to. To her astonishment, Kate shrugged.

"I don't know," she said. "What do you want to do? What do you want?"

"Funny, I was just asking myself that. A tranquil family life. Happy, thriving kids. A healthy, loving relationship with my husband. And I also want passion. Passion for something that has nothing to do with them."

"I think," Kate said, hesitating a little, "that all these things should be possible in a life. And if for some reason they are not, you have a decision to make. It's not a decision between your husband and an art class. You realize that, don't you?"

Sophie must have looked confused, because Kate repeated the question.

"It's more about what the art class represents. You want to do something for yourself and Alex isn't really behind it. And you've decided to go for it anyway, despite his objections. But you have to figure out if you can accept that he's not okay with it. That's more the issue, don't you think?"

"To be honest, this whole issue is beyond me right now." Sophie waited for Kate to jump in, but Kate said nothing. She was sipping her tea, looking at Sophie, letting her speak.

❖

Hours later, Sophie was still thinking about her friend's visit. As she lay on the sofa waiting for the kids to come home she repeated Kate's words aloud and gently tapped her forehead. She'd been seeing the world in terms of either/or. Husband or art class. Kate was right. There was so much more to it. And for once, Kate did not have all the answers. Instead, she left Sophie with even more questions. And something else. She opened her hand and let the crystal dangle. It glistened in the late afternoon sunshine, which streamed in through the window. Kate's story of how it had passed from woman to woman had made Sophie cry. She could only hope that it would help her too.

CHAPTER 29

SARAH

Sarah was sitting in her office and had spent the past fifteen minutes trying to muddle through an article. She reread the first sentence five times and still could not absorb it. She closed her eyes and visualized Mia's crystal hoping it would bring her some serenity. The calm that had returned to her life had been short-lived when, four days ago, everything changed. Sarah tried not to allow her tumultuous home life to affect her work and patients, but it was taking every bit of energy for her to focus on them.

"Sarah! Where are you?" Sarah jumped and looked up.

"Gina, you scared me half to death."

"Are you all right? You were definitely somewhere else just now."

"I'm fine."

"I just wanted to let you know that I'm going to have to leave a bit early today."

"Uh-huh."

"You sure you're all right? Is there anything I can do?"

"I'll see you tomorrow," Sarah said, ignoring the question.

Sarah didn't want to talk about this with Gina. Or most anyone else, for that matter. No, this discussion she was saving for Mia, which made getting through today all the more difficult. Sarah glanced at the clock, then stared, watching the minutes tick away at what seemed like a snail's pace. Five o'clock would never come. She and Mia had agreed to meet downstairs in the hospital atrium before Mia's interview with Kate. Sarah couldn't wait. They had been in touch over the phone about a month ago but they hadn't seen each other since that day in the coffee shop.

There was so much to tell her. Sarah tried to organize it, knowing that her words would likely spill out in a rush of disjointed thoughts. Mia knew that she and Matthew had decided to adopt. She knew that they were searching in China. She knew that they had been buried under mounds of paperwork. She knew that there had been a home assessment. She did not know about the recent events that had derailed her.

Sarah was sitting at a table in the atrium at five o'clock on the nose. A frazzled Mia ran in fifteen minutes later, offering an apology and a complaint about the terrible parking around the hospital. She sat down opposite and Sarah exhaled. She took one of Sarah's hands and clutched it for half a minute before letting go.

"How *are* you?" she asked.

"Good," Sarah said, with an involuntary quiver in her voice. Mia heard it.

"Uh-huh," Mia said, though it sounded like a question. Her brow furrowed. "What's going on?"

"Well, there's been a bit of a change of plans." Sarah inhaled and launched into an account of the week.

Just after her last phone call with Mia, she and Matthew had wrestled with yet another impossible decision. Sarah had been calling the adoption agency repeatedly. She knew the number now by heart. Matthew chided her but was also mildly amused. "Maybe you should give them a call and ask if there's a particular brand of diaper that we should be using. Maybe Chinese kids have different needs for their butts," he said one evening as she jotted down another question.

"Ha ha. Hilarious."

During one call, Sarah asked about the wait. In the absence of an answer that would be different from the one that had been offered countless times, the agency worker suggested an option that would speed up the process. It had been proposed to Sarah and Matthew at the very first meeting but they had refused it.

"Remember that if you're open to accepting a child with special needs, the wait is shorter. But we would have to conduct a psychiatric evaluation."

"What does that mean, exactly, *special needs*?"

"It means that they have some sort of medical condition or problem. Some are more serious than others. Some can be treated. Some cannot. We would ask you what you would be comfortable with, what you wouldn't be comfortable with. And then, when a child became available we would let you know and you would have the option of accepting him or her, or not."

"You mean we could reject a baby because he or she is too sick?" As a nurse, Sarah had learned to maintain a sense of calm on matters related to illness. She had seen so much, witnessed the challenges that so many of her patients had lived with or overcome, and yet, as she contemplated such a harrowing decision, she imagined how heartbreaking it would be to make that choice.

"Yes."

She had thought the soul-searching for her and Matthew was behind them. But yet again, they found themselves back in it. This time, Matthew was the one with reservations, raising all the questions that Sarah had considered herself. They were all valid. Their families wanted to be supportive but were concerned about the toll that a child with a disability might have on them. What it came down to was this: what medical conditions did they think they could take on, financially and emotionally? She did not want to convince him. She simply appealed to his pragmatic nature and then let him come to his own conclusion.

"It's not as if we're making an irreversible decision. We can go step-by-step. If a child is presented to us and we feel that we can't undertake the responsibility, for whatever reason, then we don't."

It made sense, but Sarah still understood the pained look on Matthew's face. Not moving forward meant that they would be turning down a child because they couldn't manage his or her health problems. She was a nurse, after all. Shouldn't she, of all people, be able to deal with this? It would be an agonizing choice. On the other hand, being closed to adopting a child with special needs meant that they were pre-emptively rejecting all of them. And that thought ultimately helped make up their minds.

Sarah had thought that she would have a bit of time to think, but two weeks later they got the call. A baby was available. He had a cleft lip and palate but was healthy in all other respects. Sarah and Matthew had forty-eight hours to decide if this was their child. That it was a boy was completely unexpected and both were excited, though no more than they would have been had it been a girl. Sarah immediately called a doctor that she knew at the hospital and Matthew jumped on the Internet. What they both discovered was that this was a problem that could be corrected, but that there could be certain residual issues, like speech or dental problems. With just their gut feeling and the information they had, Sarah and Matthew were ready to make their decision.

Mia was staring in amazement. "Oh my God, what did you do?"

Sarah smiled and opened her purse. She pulled out a photo and slid it across the table.

"Mia, meet my son."

CHAPTER 30

MIA

The photo filled her with both joy and anguish.

As Mia stared at the face of the nine-month-old boy, she felt exhilarated to know that what had to be a bleak and lonely existence would soon be replaced with a life full of love and hope. She looked, with some discomfort, at the gaping space where part of his upper lip should have been, but the slight upward turn of the corner of his mouth made Mia smile right back at him. This little boy with spiky, black hair and dark eyes did not yet know how lucky he was. He did not know that in a few short months his parents would be coming to get him. Sarah had already found every possible piece of information about surgically correcting the cleft lip and palate and, in her words, had cornered a couple of doctors at the hospital to ask for guidance.

Mia could not think of a woman who deserved this more than Sarah. Sarah had told Mia that she often felt that tug of fear, but that if she succumbed to it, it would consume her and she would feel little else. Instead, she moved forward despite the uncertainty that would now be part of her and Matthew's lives.

And anguish. Mia was usually able to live with the fact that she did not know when – or if – she would be a mother. But this ability was not an armoured cloak. Every wedding or baby announcement that came from a friend still felt like a dagger to the heart.

When Mia and Sarah were in the car together on their way to Kate's for the interview, Sarah apologized for monopolizing the conversation. "I'm so sorry," she said. "This has all been me, me, me. What's going on in your life?"

"I do have some news myself."

"You met someone!" Mia knew that Sarah meant well, but that sort of thing drove her nuts.

"Um, no."

"Sorry. I'm such an idiot. What's your news?"

"I'm moving," Mia said.

"You're what?" Sarah took her eyes off the road and glanced at Mia, and in that brief moment, Mia thought she saw dread.

"To New York, to NYU, to do a master's degree in journalism."

"That's great," Sarah said, her tone flat with disappointment.

Mia ignored it. "It's always been in my plan to do a master's degree. I need to shake things up a bit right now. I need a change. But I'm pretty terrified." She stared through the car window watching the cars whiz by in the other direction. She thought about what the new landscape might look like. Buried deep beneath the angst, she knew there was excitement and anticipation. She just had to connect with those sentiments. A new city, fresh faces, a different routine. Or no routine. That's what she needed. She had always thought that she was too soft for a place like New York City. Mia pictured herself splayed on the grimy sidewalk at 42nd and Broadway, literally trampled by the frantic pace of one of the greatest and harshest cities she knew. The image made her laugh.

Since she had announced her decision, her mother had repeatedly said that she could always come home. She had moments when she felt physically ill, and in those moments she was unsure whether she would be capable of leaving. She tried not to think of her sister's kids.

"Seriously, I am happy for you," Sarah said, trying to sound positive.

"I know you are. And this doesn't mean that we won't talk to each other and see each other," Mia said, speaking aloud Sarah's worry.

"Can I call you whenever I think I'm screwing up my kid?"

"You can call me," Mia said, "but I don't know how much help I'll be."

"When are you leaving?" Sarah asked as they turned onto Kate's street. "I think this is the house," she said before Mia could glance at the piece of paper with Kate's address. Sarah pulled up to the curb and turned the ignition off.

"In a month."

"And you're still doing this piece on cancer?" The two women walked up the path to the door and Sarah rang the bell.

"It's my last assignment," Mia said. The door opened and Kate flung her arms around Sarah.

Their hostess ushered them into the living room where another woman waited for them. "I hope you don't mind," Kate said. "I've asked my friend Sophie if she would be here today. She went through some of this with me and will probably be able to remind me of things I may have forgotten."

"I don't mind at all," Mia said, shaking Sophie's hand. "It will be helpful to get your perspective."

"And I asked Angel to come for moral support," Kate said, slipping her arm around Sarah's waist.

"Angel?" Mia questioned.

"That's what her patients call her," Kate answered. Sarah grinned in embarrassment.

Kate served tea and the four of them settled into two sofas facing one another. All eyes turned to Mia who was fumbling with the audio recorder on her phone. "Kate," she said when she finally had it running, "let's start with the facts: when and how you were diagnosed, your surgery, your treatment plan, the timeline—"

The women turned to Kate as she detailed her experience. Mia jotted down notes and Sarah and Sophie listened, sipping from steaming cups. When she was done, Mia turned the page in her notebook and continued. "So you've finished your treatment?"

"Yes," Kate said.

"Would you say that you beat cancer?" Mia asked.

"I won this round. That much I can say."

"What is life like after cancer, Kate? Are you constantly worrying that it will come back or are you able to resume your life as it was before?"

Kate looked at Sarah and Sophie. Then she launched into an account of the scare she'd recently had and the solace she found in a support group. Kate suddenly went silent and Mia looked up from her notebook to see that she was dabbing at her eyes with a tissue.

"Those women," she said. "Godsends. Every one of them. Which is appropriate, since Angel is the one who brought them to me." Kate turned to Angel. "Anyone can imagine what it must be like to face cancer, but until you do, you can never truly understand." Then she turned to Sophie. "You've been amazing, Sophie, it's just that—"

"It's fine, Kate. I understand what you mean," Sophie said.

"So what did these women bring you that others couldn't?" Mia asked.

"They helped me cope better. I thought I was coping well but, as it turns out, I wasn't doing such a great job. I don't have to think twice about what I am saying to them. I don't have to worry about protecting them from the ugliness of this disease. It took a session or two, but now I'm able to say whatever I'm thinking and feeling, no matter how irrational it is. And they empathize."

It was comforting for Mia to hear about another person's

struggle and victory over the fears imposed by an unpredictable future.

When Kate was done, Mia turned to Sophie. "What has been your role?"

"I don't know if I had a role," Sophie said.

"Her role was vital," Kate said. "She put up with me."

"I was there to listen. But I have to say that more often than not, Kate would want to talk about anything but her cancer. She would usually change the subject. She wanted to know what was going on in my life. I think I dumped more on her than she dumped on me. I feel bad about that."

Kate shook her head. "It was what I needed at the time. I was just so bloody sick of myself."

"But when Kate did want to talk, I let her. I tried to steer clear of telling her what to do, or telling her how to feel. I didn't judge."

"Yeah, she did what I have never been able to do," Kate added, looking sheepish.

"The truth is," Sophie continued, ignoring Kate's interjections, "I learned so much from her throughout this process. I'm starting to realize that her cancer has had a profound effect on me."

"How so?" Mia asked.

"I watched her live through the hardest fight of her life. And she did it with such grace."

"Hardly," Kate said, her face going pink.

Once again, Sophie ignored her. "So I said to myself, 'If she can face this disease, then I can face whatever comes my way.' She gives me courage to move forward."

"Really?" Kate interrupted again.

"I was going to say all this to you. But this story isn't about me."

"Actually, your experience could be useful for the article. If you don't mind, that is," Mia said.

"Oh," Sophie said hesitantly. "I suppose it would be okay, though I wouldn't want my husband to be able to identify me in print. Not that he will read this article."

"I can keep the details non-specific," Mia reassured.

Sophie talked about her marriage, how stifled she had felt. She had tried to find outlets for her creativity and energy, but it hadn't worked out.

"So I suppose that watching Kate deal with her cancer helped me to deal with my own stuff. Plus, her blunt opinions didn't fall on deaf ears even though I sometimes wished I were deaf." She and Kate laughed. "And of course, my daughter played an important role. Both my kids, really. I wasn't setting a very good example by hiding in a broken marriage and disregarding my own needs. So I finally took a stand."

"I don't believe it. You left him!" Kate squealed.

"No, Kate," Sophie said, her voice edging towards exasperation. "I didn't leave him. I got a job. I'm working as an administrative assistant at an art gallery."

Kate looked confused. "But that must be killing Alex. He won't like it one bit. How does that resolve anything?"

"He wasn't thrilled, that's for sure. And it doesn't resolve anything completely. But that's just it. For now I can live with non-resolution. And I am earning money so I can be more independent. I'm learning about the art world, hoping that eventually I can do something a bit more stimulating there. And, if at some point in the future, the situation with Alex becomes untenable, then maybe I'll—. We'll see. I'll figure it out."

Kate grinned. "You know what, Sophie? I'm happy for you." Sophie reached over to squeeze Kate's hand and as she did, the pendant swung forward in plain view.

Mia froze. The women were looking at her, waiting for her next question.

"That necklace—" she started. "Where did you get it?" Mia glanced over at Sarah, who had leaned forward for a better look. Sarah's eyes went wide as well.

"Kate gave it to me," Sophie said. And as she did, Mia saw before her the path that her crystal had taken.

"It actually has a beautiful story," Sophie continued, and then stopped short. She stared into Mia's eyes. "Wait, is this yours?"

"I believe it is! I gave it to Sarah." Mia scanned the faces of the three women, watching as they absorbed what was unfolding in the room. No one wanted to be the first to speak. Finally, Sophie turned to Kate.

"I have had this crystal for only a couple of weeks, but it has meant more to me than you could know." She reached behind her neck to unhook the clasp, then placed it in the palm of her hand and rubbed its surface. "But I think it can now be returned to its owner." Holding each end of the silver chain, Sophie stood up and walked over to Mia, who lifted her hair.

"It's in its rightful place," Sarah said as Sophie attached it around Mia's neck. "You need it now. You can think of each one of us as you start this next chapter."

Mia could not speak. When she found her voice some minutes later, she told them she had enough for her article. Still, none of the women moved. Kate finally broke the silence by suggesting they have a glass of wine together on her deck. The three women followed Kate through her kitchen toward the patio doors and stepped out into the sunlight.

ACKNOWLEDGEMENTS

The seed for this story was planted at the 50th birthday party of my dear friend, Joanne Besner. A simple gesture that evening morphed into what became an eight-year-long writing journey replete with exhilaration and excitement, as well as frustration and self-doubt. During those moments, Joanne and countless friends and family members provided support and encouragement that ultimately led to the birth of *The Prague Crystal*. To them, I owe a debt of gratitude.

In particular, two extraordinary women accompanied me on this adventure from the very first word to the last, advising me, editing multiple versions of the manuscript, agonizing over punctuation and adverbs, and generally propelling me forward. To Pam Orzeck and Wendy Singer, *The Prague Crystal* is a joint achievement. Thank you for your unwavering commitment to this project.

In writing this novel, I tackled subjects and issues that were foreign to me and I was fortunate to have a team of people who were at the ready, willing to share their stories. Thank you to Lisa Dalcourt, Deborah Bridgman, Romy Schnaiberg and Amy Eini, warriors in their own right. Thank you to the friends and friends of friends who allowed me access to their personal lives, and to Hinda Goodman from Hope & Cope at the Jewish General Hospital for the information and resources. All were instrumental in helping me capture the emotional realities of my characters and ensure accuracy. If there are any errors in any of the medical details or those related to fertility or adoption, they are mine alone.

Thank you to the Humber School for Writers and to my author-mentor, Sarah Sheard, for elevating the first draft of the manuscript, to Claire Holden Rothman for the meticulous edits and invaluable guidance, and to Allen Zuk for leading the way to publication.

I thank Josie Gold for her beautiful artistry, Lucy Barylak for helping me achieve my first publishing credit, and Caitlin Alifirenka and Lorraine Bloom for their time and generosity.

Through this process, I discovered how truly supportive the writing community is. Fellow writers, whose paths I happened to cross on the fleeting Twitter feed, were eager to help with advice and offers to review my writing. I am grateful to them – and, primarily, to Jamie Raintree – for their input.

Thank you to my circle of supporters who read the manuscript in its various incarnations, providing feedback and suggestions for improvements. Lastly, thank you to my parents and family, my biggest cheerleaders, who continue to believe that I can accomplish anything.